September 5

Big
Assignment

Dr. Bena R. Hartman

Author of *Jasmine Can*

FERNE PRESS

September's Big Assignment
Copyright © 2013 by Bena R. Hartman
Layout, design and cover photo by Jacqueline L. Challiss Hill
Printed in the United States of America

Summary: When fifth grader September Champlin is given a writing assignment, she has no idea how much it will affect her life.

Library of Congress Cataloging-in-Publication Data
    Hartman, Bena R.
    September's Big Assignment/Bena R. Hartman–First Edition
    ISBN-13: 978-1-938326-10-3
    1. Juvenile fiction. 2. Elementary school. 3. Aliteracy. 4. Families. 5. Friendship.
    I. Hartman, Bena R. II. Title
    Library of Congress Control Number: 2012951880

FERNE PRESS

Ferne Press is an imprint of Nelson Publishing & Marketing
366 Welch Road, Northville, MI 48167
www.nelsonpublishingandmarketing.com
(248) 735-0418

Other Books by Bena R. Hartman
Jasmine Can: Creating Self-Confidence

This book is dedicated
to the memory of my father,
who lived unselfishly,
who embraced life to the fullest, and
who encouraged me beyond words.

BH

I wish to thank my publisher, Marian Nelson, and editor, Kris Yankee, for their unfailing leadership on this project; colleagues from the University of South Florida, Dr. James King, and the University of Pittsburgh, Dr. Rita Bean, for providing their expertise in literacy education; Dr. George Zimmerman, also from the University of Pittsburgh, for his insights on visual impairments; friends Charla Yingling, Lisa Henry, Katie Davis, and Eric Bernard; teachers Christena Sinila, Jennifer Eddy, and Marcie Abdullah; pastor Dr. Richard Allen Farmer; my mother, Ruth Hefflin; my brother Dr. Brockton Hefflin; and my husband, Dr. Douglas Hartman, for contributing immeasurable feedback in the areas of their expertise. Much thanks also to my children, Vail, Laya, and Bethany, who always remind me to say things the way a child would say them and stuff. I would also like to acknowledge the historians at Pittsburgh's Neighbors in the Strip for providing a historical overview of the Strip District. Finally, I would like to pay tribute to all the children's authors whose books are mentioned in the story. Thank you for writing entertaining stories that delight my soul.

BH

Chapter 1

The Diamond-Studded READ Pin

Read? Over the summer? That's a dumb question. I didn't read any books over the summer. I can't speak for anyone else, but I read when I have to, like for an assignment or when I'm on the Internet or something. I don't read on rainy days, on the weekends, when I'm bored, and especially not during the summer. My point is, I *can* read. I just choose not to, that's all.

I slip my hand up. "I didn't read any books over the summer, Mrs. Bridgewaters. Were we supposed to?" I ask politely.

A few kids snicker, while Real-to-Real and Deshawn, the class clowns, laugh out loud. Mrs. Bridgewaters slants her eyes and gives them the *don't-you-laugh-like-that-in-my-classroom* stare. It worked 'cause they stop laughing as quickly as they started.

"Well, of course you were, September," Mrs. Bridgewaters replies with a smile, while straightening the diamond-studded READ pin on her turquoise blouse.

It's quiet in here. Everyone's beady little eyeballs are glued directly on me. What? I don't like to read, okay? If I don't like to read, I'm definitely not gonna do it over summer vacation. The summer's a time to relax, chill, have fun with friends and family. Not a time to

1

read a bunch of boring books. And another thing, if I were brave, I would say all this out loud.

"It's pretty clear that reading enhances your imagination, broadens your vocabulary, and strengthens your comprehension," Mrs. Bridgewaters continues. "Reading empowers you, makes you smarter," she says while tapping her finger on the side of her forehead.

Hold up. *Is she trying to say that I'm not smart?* But then, she wouldn't be the first. I tell myself that all the time.

"It's also fun to do. I love curling up on my sofa with a hot cup of coffee and a good book. It's relaxing." Mrs. Bridgewaters winks at me before moving on. "How about others? What books did you read over the summer?"

Everybody raises their hands. You mean to tell me *I* was the only one who didn't read this summer? That's embarrassing. Even the *boys* raised their hands, including Real-to-Real. And here I thought he was an airhead like me. Real-to-Real's first name is actually Houston. But I call him Real-to-Real because he's either real nice or real silly or real loud or real crazy-acting with a real flat head 'n stuff.

"I see we had lots of readers this summer." Mrs. Bridgewaters has a huge smile on her face. "Who would like to begin?" She looks around the room. "Let's see. Sabeen, I saw your hand first."

"I kept a journal of all the books I read and wrote a summary about each one."

"Oh brother," I say, rolling my eyes and slapping my forehead.

"I also critiqued each book."

She did *what*?

"I read twenty novels and two books on string theory."

I'm looking at Sabeen all bug-eyed. What's string theory?

"My favorite novel was *Jacob Have I Loved* by Katherine Paterson. String theory is…"

"Oh, I love that story!" Yuan shouts out, cutting Sabeen off. "The grandmother in that story was mean! Especially when she said, 'Jacob have I loved. Esau have I hated.' I'm glad she's not my grandmother."

Everyone starts laughing, including Mrs. Bridgewaters. For the next twenty-five minutes or so, my mind is half-listening to my classmates talk about the books they read over the summer and half-feeling sorry for myself because I can't be part of the discussion. I feel left out for sure. The thing is, I hate reading. Hate it, hate it, hate it! How am I going to become a reader like Mrs. Bridgewaters wants me to if I don't like to read?

Here's why I don't like it: I'll start reading a story and then lose interest. Before I know it, I've read an entire page and don't remember what I read 'cause I was thinking about something else. Then I have to go back and read it all over again, forcing myself to pay attention to something that I was never interested in reading in the first place. That frustrates me, and *that's* why I don't like to read! And *that's* why I'll never become a *real* reader.

"There's a stack of chapter books by my favorite author, Virginia Hamilton, on the floor next to my nightstand waiting to be read," Diamond says. "I have *Zeely*, and *M. C. Higgins, the Great...*"

There's a stack of books on my floor, too. Picture books by Dr. Seuss. They've been there going on two, three years now. I flip through them every once in a while.

"*The Phantom Tollbooth* was so good I read it twice," says Braden.

I have better things to do with my time—like watch TV, listen to music, hang out with my friends, and watch more TV—than to sit around and read a stupid book.

"When we went to Florida I took *Bud, Not Buddy* with me and finished it before we came back to Pittsburgh," says Kendrick.

He took a book with him on a trip? Who does that?

"By a show of hands, who takes a book with them on a trip?" Mrs. Bridgewaters asks.

Half of the kids raise their hands. Mrs. Bridgewaters raises her hand, too.

"Not bad. But it's not *good* either. My goal is for everyone's hand to be raised. I want a community of readers, students who read all the time, not just when they're told to. You see, I look at each and every one of you like you're a work in progress or a fine piece of silver that needs to be polished and smoothed o'er. When silver has been carefully tended to, it radiates and shines just like the ball

3

of fire up in the sky. Looks like I have my work cut out for me this year," she says, smiling at me. Instead of smiling back, I look down at my desk and try hard not to cry.

"Okay, class. Let's switch gears. As promised, here's your last assignment for the day," she says while passing it out.

"I've certainly enjoyed getting to know you this first week of school, but I'd like to know more. I created this assignment to help me get to know you better. Read and follow the directions. Use the checklist on the back as a guide for your writing. You'll use a checklist like this throughout the year for all your writing assignments, so get used to it. I'll tweak it, that is, change it based on the writing purpose. This'll take a few days to complete. Brainstorm your ideas first. Don't rush to get it done. It takes time to write. Any questions?" Mrs. Bridgewaters scans the room. "Ajala?"

"Can we type the final copy or does it have to be handwritten?"

"I'd like it to be handwritten. Use your best writing," Mrs. Bridgewaters says in a motherly voice.

"How long does it have to be?" asks Jamal.

"Long enough to cover the topic, but short enough to keep my interest. That translates to two to three pages," she says smiling while holding up three fingers. "Tori?"

"I have *way* more than three talents. Should I write about them all?"

She would say that, I think to myself.

"No more than five. Is that understood, Miss Neuman?"

Tori looks disappointed, but agrees.

"Any more questions?" Mrs. Bridgewaters looks around the room.

No one raises their hand.

"Very well. You may begin."

Name:_____Date:_____

Directions: Write a friendly letter to me describing at least three (3) of your talents or best qualities. What are you good at? What do you do well? After you have written a description of your talents or best qualities, list three (3) goals that you would like to work on during the school year. Have fun with this assignment. Mrs. Bridgewaters

Three Rivers Elementary School
Grade 5
Descriptive Writing Checklist

Student_____

Bubble in each item once you have completed it.

Introduction
○ The beginning of my letter grabs the reader's attention.
○ My introductory paragraph is clearly written.
○ I explain what I am going to write about.

Organization
○ My writing is organized so that it makes sense and sounds right.
○ I use paragraphs to help organize my thoughts and ideas.
○ I use transition words so that my writing flows.
○ I avoid using the same words to begin a sentence.

Word Choice
○ I use a variety of words to make my letter interesting.
○ My writing is personal and engaging.
○ I use examples and details to explain my points.

Conventions
○ I use complete sentences.
○ My words are spelled correctly.
○ I use capitalization and punctuation correctly.
○ I use subject-verb agreement throughout my letter.
○ I use the same verb tense throughout my letter.

Overall Assignment
○ My paper is organized in letter format.
○ I write about at least three (3) of my talents or best qualities.
○ I list three (3) goals to work on during the school year.
○ I take pride in my work.

* You will not receive a letter grade for this assignment; however, you will receive credit for turning it in.

The directions say to write a letter about our talents or best qualities and list three goals to work on during the year. I have two problems with this assignment. Number one, I don't have any talents or best qualities. And number two, I don't have any goals for this year. I'm just a plain, average, eleven-year-old girl.

What the *heck* is there to write about when you see yourself as average?

There's nothing special about me. I'm not smart. I don't play any sports or instruments. I can't sing. I've never even taken hip-hop lessons. I dance at *home*, in my bedroom, when no one's watching, except for my dog, Dee-O-Gee. And he doesn't count. At least I don't *think* he does. As for best qualities, well, I am *quiet* at school. Teachers like that 'cause I don't cause them any problems.

It's probably not helpful to my classmates to be too quiet, though. Like the time in third grade when I saw Real-to-Real push Isaiah into our classroom library for no reason. All the books fell off the shelf. Isaiah got in trouble for something Real-to-Real caused and had to pick them all up. I felt sorry for Isaiah so I gave up recess that day to help him pick the books up and put them back in order, all five hundred of 'em. I thought I owed it to him since I didn't speak up and tell the teacher that it wasn't his fault. My parents were proud of me for what I did, but it doesn't take much of a *special talent* to be helpful; just someone who's kind and thoughtful is all.

I have a headache and a lump in my stomach just looking at the assignment on my desk. Maybe I can wish it away. I close my eyes: *I wish this assignment were a donut and rolled off my desk.* I open my eyes. It's still there. Let me try that again. I close my eyes and cover my face with my hands that still smell of lavender from the lotion I put on this morning. *I wish this assignment would disappear forever.* Okay, September, on the count of three open your eyes, one, two, three. I open my eyes, peek through my fingers, and look down at my desk. "Aahhh!" What a way to begin fifth grade.

Chapter 2

Three O'Clock

"Is there a problem, Miss Champlin?" Mrs. Bridgewaters asks, smiling at me and straightening the diamond-studded READ pin on her blouse, again. "Miss Champlin, are you okay?" she asks raising her voice, which she rarely does. Her words finally sink in.

"Yes, I—I—I'm okay," I stutter. I'm so frustrated over the writing assignment I can barely speak. *Can't she tell how upset I am?*

Mrs. Bridgewaters seems to be thinking over my response, rubbing her fingers lightly on her chin. She then bends down to help Real-to-Real, whose hand has been raised for a while. Guess not.

"You're off to a good start, Houston," she tells him.

Mrs. Bridgewaters has her hands on her hips as she strolls around the room in her black patent leather shoes, the kind with a flowery bow on top.

"Don't forget, boys and girls, this is not a contest to see who'll finish first. Pay close attention to all of the bullets under each heading on the checklist. Those bullets are there to help you become a thoughtful writer."

Her blue skirt sways from side to side as she passes me. *Hey airhead, ask for help*, I tell myself. Instead of listening, I take a long, deep breath and look around the room at my friends who I've known since Mrs. Sullivan's kindergarten class.

India's chomping on gum and writing as fast as the speed of light. The faster she chews, the faster she writes. *Does chewing gum help people concentrate?* If so, I want some. My guess is that the juices from the gum send tiny signals to the part of our brain that helps us come up with ideas. If that's true, I need some, now! *Yoo-hoo, In-d-ia.* I don't know why I thought that.

India can do lots of things, like match clothes. I love the orange and fuchsia outfit she's wearing today against her brown skin and all. Even the beads at the end of her braids match her outfit. But she's no mind reader. Wish she'd look my way so I can ask for a piece. It's worth a shot.

She's already on her second sheet of paper. I'm not surprised. She has tons of stuff to write about. She's *really* good at the shuttle run—she even beats the boys! And she can do fifty sit-ups in a minute. Fifty! I can barely do twenty-five. She also plays on the Elite team for soccer, basketball, and volleyball...seriously! And she's the captain on *each* team. How you get to be captain of *all* the teams you play on, I have no clue. She's always playing in a tournament and never gets to stay home and have fun with her friends. Honestly, I don't know when she sleeps. Just last week, she overheard her parents talking about her getting an athletic scholarship to some expensive university. I didn't know they gave scholarships to fifth graders. Kidding. I'm no expert, but I bet it's tough on India trying to please her parents *all* the time.

Tori—whose real name is Victoria—also has a bunch of things to write about. She's in gifted math and always has her artwork hung up in the main office. She also plays every instrument on the planet. Okay, seriously, she only plays three, but that's a lot for a ten-year-old. Tori's been playing the violin, drums, and piano ever since she was six years old! One time, I went to her piano recital. When I say *her* recital, I mean *her* recital. She was the only one in it. It lasted a whole *two hours*. I thought I was going to lose my mind, which surprised me because for the next several weeks after her recital, I hounded my parents to let me take piano lessons. That didn't last long. I learned that in order to become a good piano player, you had to practice. I found it hard finding time to practice in between waking up in the morning and going to bed at night.

Tori may be very talented, but she's also very selfish. The girl needs to learn how to think about other people's feelings for a change—put them before her own for once in her life. She's nothing like her older sister, Lizbeth, who we call Lizzie. They're about as different as night and day. Lizzie played with dolls when she was a little girl. Tori wouldn't touch them. Lizzie is friendly and outgoing; Tori's not. Lizzie likes plain cheese pizza; Tori likes onions and green peppers on hers. Blech. Lizzie's tall. Tori's short. Here's my guess: Tori was switched at birth or she was adopted and her parents haven't told her yet. Kidding, but that'll explain why she has thick, brown, curly hair, and the rest of her family has straight, blond hair. I've learned over the years there are some things I can discuss with Tori and some things I can't. And the differences between her and her sister Lizzie are some things I can't. That's fine with me. After all, she *is* my friend, and there's nothing in this world like a true friend. Right?

Tori's busy wiggling her wobbly tooth and *still* has tons of stuff written down. Her tooth would have fallen out by now if she had swapped her chocolate pudding for my apple at lunch. I tried telling her that apples are more nutritious than pudding and even stretched the truth a little when I said if she eats an apple every day, she wouldn't have to visit the dentist for a whole year. But she didn't fall for it. Who was I trying to fool? I wouldn't have fallen for it either. Besides, everybody knows you should visit the dentist at least twice a year whether you eat apples every day or not.

My eyes shift to Sabeen, my *best*, best friend. I'm closer with Sabeen than I am with India or Tori. Don't get me wrong, India and Tori are my girls, but Sabeen's my *girl*. Still, that doesn't mean we don't get on each other's nerves.

Sabeen's sitting properly in her chair with her back straight and feet flat on the floor—twirling her long brown hair with the end of her pencil every now and then. Her paper's angled in the most perfect position to help her form each letter correctly. Maybe that's

11

why her writing looks like the teachers'.

How I became best friends with the smartest fifth grader known to mankind, I'll never know. What I *do* know is that smart kids are lucky. They get lots of school privileges. Ever since kindergarten, teachers *always* choose Sabeen to do special things for them, like make photocopies, get their mail, or take notes to other teachers. Here's what else I know: Sabeen's smart because she always, I mean *always*, has her head in a book. Today is no exception. She reads in the hallways *and* during recess. She even reads walking to and from school. Why would *anyone* read a book walking to and from school? I have no clue.

Sabeen pays close attention to every little detail when she reads. Believe it or not, when Sabeen opens a book she reads the acknowledgments section first, then she reads the dedication section, and *then* she reads the publishing information. How bizarre is that? Now I can understand her reading the acknowledgments and dedication sections, but the publishing information? That's ridiculous. Who cares about the publishing information? And when she finishes the story, she always reads the summary about the author in the back of the book, or if it's an informational book, like a science textbook, she'll quiz herself on the words in the glossary. She's crazy! I mean, that information isn't even interesting. Well, at least not to me.

Sabeen's the only girl I know who likes getting books instead of cute clothes or pretty jewelry on her birthday. In fact, the only gifts she got last year were bookstore gift cards. Come to think of it, that's all she ever receives. Except for that time India accidently forgot and bought her a pink basketball that Sabeen took back the next day and used the money to buy a subscription to *National Geographic*. When I asked India how that made her feel, she told me that it hurt her feelings so I gave her a great big bear hug to cheer her up.

This year, Sabeen took it to a whole new level when she actually wanted to leave in the middle of her own party to go buy some books. I'd never buy a book for a present! I'd buy something I needed like clothes 'n candy. Somehow her mom persuaded her to stay until all her guests were gone. Sabeen was *ornery* that day, cranky and grumpy. If that's what happens to people who read as much as Sabeen reads, I never want to become a book reader—*ever*! I—just—don't—get—it! What does Sabeen find so interesting in books?

My eyes continue to wander around the room. I'm sooo frustrated! I start doodling on my paper 'cause I can't seem to find anything to write about. *Should I write about the classroom rules?* I always obey them. They must be important because we've gone over them a bazillion times this week.

I cough and sneeze on my arm instead of in my hands,
I turn my homework in on time,
I keep my hands to myself, and
I listen to others while they're speaking.

Umm, no, writing that'd be boring. Besides, lots of kids obey the classroom rules. Except for that Real-to-Real, the Classroom Library Wrecker, Bennett.

RING. Hurray! It's three o'clock. Time to go home!

"Good afternoon," Mr. Lang, the school principal, says on the loudspeaker. "Please listen carefully to today's announcements. We had an awesome first week of school! I saw many children walk in the hallways. I saw nice straight lines, and you all used your," he clears the frog in his throat and whispers, "inside voices. We kick off our biggest fundraiser of the year next week selling wrapping paper and cookie dough! Show your school spirit on Wednesday by wearing your Three Rivers Elementary School T-shirt. If you don't have one or need a bigger size, you may purchase one during lunchtime in the cafeteria on Monday. The cost is five dollars. Remember our thought for the week: *Be courteous to others.* That concludes the announcements for today. Have a happy and safe weekend. All safety patrols are on post."

While packing to go home, Mrs. Bridgewaters announces, "If you didn't finish your rough draft, that's okay. Leave your papers on your desk. You may continue when you come back on Monday. Everyone did a great job this week. Have a wonderful weekend."

My paper's covered with a bunch of doodle marks. I lay another sheet of paper on top of it 'cause I don't want anyone to know that I didn't write anything yet. As if this isn't bad enough, I watch Sabeen and Tori hand their *completed* papers to Mrs. Bridgewaters. I don't believe her; Tori's patting herself on the back.

Those airheads. They didn't even do a sloppy copy first—ugh! Okay, so they're not airheads, they're bookworms, especially Sabeen. It just feels good calling them airheads. I'd never say it to their faces; after all, they *are* my friends—even if I am a little jealous of 'em.

"Goodbye, Mrs. Bridgewaters," my friends and me say together. Or is it friends and I? Oh well, whatever. If I were a bookworm, I'd know which one is correct.

"Goodbye, ladies. Good luck at your soccer tournament this weekend, India," Mrs. Bridgwaters says, fixing her hair bun.

"Thanks."

"By the way, I've been meaning to tell you that my mother used to put my hair in that same style when I was a child. I can hear her now, 'Odessa, keep your head still. The less you squirm, the quicker we can get this done.' I didn't like to sit and get my hair braided since it took forever, but I sure liked the way it looked when she finished. She'd hand me the mirror and I'd look at myself and shake my head back. You couldn't tell me nothin'."

Mrs. Bridgewaters starts laughing and so do we—probably not for the same reason. We all look at each other like we're saying, *I didn't know Mrs. Bridgewaters's first name is Odessa.*

"September, may I have a word with you?"

What does Odessa, I mean Mrs. Bridgewaters, want with me? She walks over to her desk and I follow her.

"Correct me if I'm wrong, but I have a strong feeling that you're struggling with the writing assignment."

I can't hide anything from Mrs. Bridgewaters. "Well...I feel like I have more problems than a math book and the assignment just added one more problem."

"Let's talk about these problems of yours, September."

"What I mean is...I don't have any talents or special abilities to write about."

"Yes, you do." She lifts my chin. "You, my dear, don't know what

14

they are. Don't worry. It's my job to help you discover them. Here's what I'd like you to do this weekend."

What? She's giving me homework to do? I shoulda pretended I was sick today.

"I want you to think about all the things you've done for people over the years. Make a mental record of them. In addition, keep track of everything you do this weekend. Take note of all the activities you engage in and everything you do for others, too. For example, if you help your mom wash the dishes, put that down. Make a list in your head. Better yet, write it down on this." She reaches toward her desk and hands me a notebook. "I'm going to set aside some time on Monday for the two of us to examine what you've written."

This is unusual. No teacher has *ever* paid this much attention to *me* before.

"I'll bet your notebook will be full of things you didn't realize were talents. After we review your list, we'll come up with some goals to work on during the year. Does that sound reasonable?"

It's quiet for a moment. "I think so," I answer slowly. That's what I *say*. It's not how I *feel*.

"Good deal," she replies with a big grin, then points to her diamond-studded READ pin like it's a piece of gold.

Mrs. Bridgewaters has an annoying habit of pointing to her pin to encourage us to read at home. I got news for you, sista. Reading's just not my thing, and with so many other interesting things to do at home, it's gonna take more than pointing to a silly pin to get *me* to read outside of school.

Chapter 3

Mrs. Bridgewaters

Other than that annoying gesture Mrs. Bridgewaters does with her pin, I really like her. I even accidently called her "Mom" today. Something tells me Mrs. Bridgewaters is going to be my favorite teacher. She's always smiling, she doesn't yell at us, and she even plays with us during recess. Yesterday a bunch of us were playing Double Dutch jump rope when Mrs. Bridgewaters asked if she could play. I thought it was going to be funny to watch her jump, but I was w-r-o-n-g, wrong! She's gotta be pushin' sixty-five, but *honey*, can she jump. I was surprised she could move that fast. I hate to admit it, but she was better than us. When the other kids saw what she was doing, they gathered around and started to chant, "Go, Mrs. B! Go, Mrs. B!" That whole jump rope experience put her at the top of my teacher list for sure!

Or maybe she's at the top of my list because she tells us stories about her life that make me feel sorry for her.

"Back when I was a little girl I was fat growing up and was teased a lot by other kids," she said.

Now in some teachers' classrooms, believe it or not, kids would have howled in their seats, making "oink" sounds if a teacher told a story like that. But not in Mrs. Bridgewaters's room. We showed her respect by listening. I will admit, I looked at Mercedes, who's at least twenty or so pounds overweight, when Mrs. Bridgewaters said the word "fat" to get Mercedes' reaction. She sat motionless, like a statue the whole time while staring big-eyed at Mrs. Bridgewaters. I'm so tempted to ask her how she feels when people say the word "fat" around her, but that seems rude, so I'll do like Grandma Lipscomb says and keep my thoughts to myself.

"On my tenth birthday, I invited my whole class to my party and no one came, not even my own father. The only person who showed up was my teacher, Mrs. Harris, whom I loved like my own mother. Mrs. Harris had a saying: 'Dream big dreams, and they'll take you far in life.'"

Mrs. Bridgewaters never forgot about Mrs. Harris, or her saying. In fact, she said it to us throughout this first week of school and even wrote it on our papers. She wrote other things, too, like *Way to go* and *Good work* in fancy handwriting. But I liked when she wrote the saying best because it made me feel like I could do anything. Mrs. Bridgewaters is so good at what she does that at one point she almost had me believing I could actually become a reader! Me? A reader?

Mrs. Bridgewaters is the kind of teacher who goes out of her way to help students, even if they're not in her classroom. I remember when a really poor family came to our school last year, seven children in all. Four of them were girls. They didn't have any pretty dresses or shoes to wear to our Winter Concert. Mrs. Bridgewaters bought the girls new dresses and shoes with her *own* money. She even paid for them to get their hair done at the beauty salon. The girls ended up looking better than all the other girls in the program. When Tori saw how nice they looked, she glanced at me and said, "I wish I was poor." I couldn't believe she said that. I wanted to nail her mouth shut and lecture her about how good her life was compared to theirs, but the concert was about to begin so I rolled my eyes at her instead. *She'll eat those words some day,* I thought. "Choose your battles," Grandma Lipscomb says. That was one battle not worth fighting. Maybe there will be some day, but that wasn't the day.

Mrs. Bridgewaters is also the type of teacher who goes to school early and stays late. I know she goes early because my dad sees her car at school on his way to work. I know she stays late because he sees her car parked in the same spot on his way home from work. Sometimes she even goes in on the weekends! One time on our way home from the grocery store, we stopped to help her carry some boxes into her room. The box my dad carried had an aquarium for her classroom pets. It had two gerbils in it that she named Winter and Solstice.

Maybe she spends so much time at school because she doesn't have any children to take care of at home anymore. Or maybe she's lonely since her husband, Judge Bridgewaters, died a couple years ago. I met him before. He used to help Mrs. Bridgewaters hang stuff up in her room. And he'd read stories to us during special times, like America Reads and Martin Luther King Jr. Day.

I'll never forget the time he read a story about Ruby Bridges. She was the very first black child to go to an all-white elementary school in the South way back in 1960 during the civil rights movement. The story he read was really sad. While he was reading, I tried imagining myself as Ruby walking up to the school surrounded by police and all those angry white people. I was like, wow…she seems so brave! I don't think I would've been that brave. I wondered what made her so brave. The story didn't say.

When he finished reading, Judge Bridgewaters closed the book very softly. Part of me wished he had never opened it in the first place. Later that day Sabeen asked me, "Did you like the story?"

I told her, "Yes, because I liked the pictures."

Before I could even get the words, "Did you like it?" off my tongue, she gave me the strangest look—a blank stare, then slowly stuck a carrot stick in her mouth and raised her book in front of her face. A few seconds went by before she tipped her book to the side to see if I was still looking at her. I was. She quickly put her book in front of her face again.

I had no idea why she did that. She was acting weird, so I came right out and asked, "Did you like it, too?"

She didn't respond right away, but I knew she heard me.

"I've had it up to here playing games, Sabeen," I said, raising my hand above my head. I started walking away.

"The story touched my mind and my heart. It was sad, yet powerful. I liked it a lot!" she said.

I stopped and looked over my shoulder at Sabeen, my mouth slightly open.

"That's it? That's what I wasted my time for! For you, the smartest kid ever, a never-stop-reading-always-keep-learning genius to say. What am I complaining about? For once you said something that I totally understand *and* agree with. I'm glad you didn't say it in French."

We were both silent for a minute, and then we busted out laughing.

During another visit, Judge Bridgewaters talked about all the famous African Americans he knew from Pittsburgh, like August Wilson, the man who wrote a lot of famous plays, like *The Piano Lesson*. I remembered his name 'cause he's named after a month like me. I wanted to ask him a question at the end of another talk, but I was too shy to raise my hand and ask in front of everyone, so I waited until we were on our way out of the auditorium.

"Judge Bridgewaters," I said quietly, "did you *really* know Martin Luther King Jr. *and* Rosa Parks?"

"'Deed I did, little lady." He continued nodding his head and said while laughing, "Deed—I—did."

Another time he talked about what it was like growing up in Pittsburgh in the 1940s. His experience sort of reminded me of the story about Ruby Bridges.

"Pittsburgh," he said, "was Seg-re-ga-tion City."

I'm glad I wasn't living back then. Things seem so different now. I wonder...*would I have been friends with all my friends back then?* I mean, I know I would've been friends with Sabeen; she's biracial, like me. She's part Asian and part black; I'm black and white; and India's all black. But Tori's all white. *Would we have been friends? Could I have been friends with a white girl?*

I'll say this for Pittsburgh: it's a great place to grow up now. And Squirrel Hill, where we live, is especially nice. It's mainly a white,

Jewish community, but there are lots of people like Asian Americans, African Americans, and East Indians mixed in. The neighbors are friendly and keep the neatest yards, there're a ton of kids, and there're lots of good places to eat, like Napoli's, and fun places to play, like Frick Park.

Moving on, I guess Mrs. Bridgewaters's hard work was worth it, though. Last year she won the Teacher of the Year Award and got to meet the president of the United States. I wish I could meet the president one day. Sometimes, I daydream about what it would be like being president, and then I wake up and convince myself I'm crazy for thinking I could possibly *be* president.

The most obvious reason it's crazy for me to think I could possibly be president is because I'm black, and let's be honest, this country's not ready for a black president, at least not in my lifetime anyway. And maybe not even the one after that, and the one after that. Another reason why it's crazy for me to think I can be president is because I'm a girl and there's never been a girl president before. I don't think there's been a girl president because when you're elected to be president your hair immediately turns gray, and what girl in her right mind wants to have gray hair? My mom doesn't. I'd rather be the president's wife so I can sit back and order people around all day with my naturally colored hair. The last reason why it's crazy for me to think I can be president is because I'm not a reader and everybody knows the president has to read a lot to know a lot. Or hire a bunch of smart people to help him run the country. That counts me out, too!

Chapter 4

Saved by the Car Horn

I hold the door open for my friends on our way out of school 'cause their hands are full, as usual. India has her soccer book of drills and plays. Tori has her piano books. She's holding the books with one hand and pretending to play the piano with the other. And Sabeen's reading a book—no surprise there! Only this time, she almost walks right into the door.

"Sabeen, watch out!"

"Merci beaucoup—thank you very much," she says passing me.

"You're welcome."

I'm nearly through the door when something very large catches my eyes. It's the new TV monitor that Mr. Clark, our school custodian, just installed. I stop and read the school motto on the screen— *At Three Rivers Elementary School we enter to do our best and we leave to help others.* I never thought much about our school motto before, but for some strange reason I think about what it means for a moment today.

When I get outside, my friends are almost around the corner. They must've run some of the way.

"Guys, wait up!" I shout, catching up to them. "Hey India," I say, out of breath, "can I have a piece of gum?"

"*May* I have a piece of gum?" Sabeen says. I hate it when she corrects me. I ignore her and keep my focus on India, hoping she'll say yes.

India says, "Sure." She grabs her bottom lip and pulls it out. This makes Tori laugh. Sabeen's too busy to notice. I stop walking, cross my arms, and stare at her until she answers me nicely.

"What?" she says playfully. "You asked for some gum."

"Girl, please. You know what I mean. Chewing gum, not the gum in your mouth that's connected to your teeth."

"Sorry, I don't have any more," she says, shrugging her shoulders and continuing to walk.

Dang. Looks like I'll have to wait to test my hypothesis to see if gum chewing helps people to concentrate. On second thought, maybe there's nothing scientific about gum chewing at all and India's gum is just plain magic. I throw my hands up in frustration and continue walking, too.

India reaches up and smacks a bunch of dried leaves hanging from a tree with her soccer book.

"What'd you guys write for your talents or best qualities?" she asks.

Tori looks at India. "What do you think I wrote about?" she says, pointing to her piano books. "I'm an awesome musician, so I wrote about all the instruments I play. I also wrote about how good I am in math," she says confidently, rubbing her tongue against her wobbly tooth while pushing her lip forward.

"I knew you were gonna say that," India says, stepping on some leaves. "I love sports, so I wrote about all the sports I play."

I bend down, pick up a bunch of reddish leaves, and crinkle them in my hand.

"What'd you write about, Sabeen?" India asks, picking up her pace then leaping over a stick like a hurdler.

She doesn't answer her right away. By the look on her face, Sabeen seems uninterested in being a part of our conversation. Then, without lifting her head from her book, Sabeen says, "I wrote about the times I won spelling bee contests, essay contests, and when I appeared on that TV show a couple years ago, *How Smart Is Your Third Grader?"*

Does she always have to sound so grown up?

I pucker my lips and blow the crumbled leaves from my hand and watch them fall rapidly to the ground. What comes next shocks us all. Sabeen gets her nose out of her book! Then she sticks her finger in the book to keep her place.

"Guess what's waiting for me when I get home?" she asks.

"What?" we shout.

"A kitten. I got him last night."

"Awww," we say.

"What's his name?" I ask.

"I haven't named him yet."

"What color is he?" asks India, leaping over another stick.

"He's black and white."

"Why didn't you tell us earlier?" India asks, picking up the stick.

"I wanted to finish reading this chapter. It's fascinating!" Sabeen says, smiling and staring at her book like she's in some sort of a trance.

We all look at each other, then crack up laughing. Even Sabeen. Then she starts reading her book again.

"What did you write about, September?" India asks, whirling back and throwing the stick on the Yangs' freshly mowed lawn.

I search my brain to come up with an excuse, but I can't think of anything. I'm forced to tell the truth. As I open my mouth to say that I didn't write anything yet, *honk, honk,* my mom sounds the horn and drives up alongside us just in the nick of time. I'm saved by the car horn.

"Hello, ladies," she says.

"Hi, Mrs. Champlin."

"Would anyone like a ride home?"

"No, thanks. I'm going to Desiree's house," says India. "She lives on Monitor, not too far down. Her mother's driving us to soccer practice. Don't forget my tournament's at two o'clock on Sunday at Schenely Oval. See you guys there."

"Bye, India," Tori says.

"Bye, Tori."

"See you on Sunday," I say.

"Okay!" India shouts over her shoulder, turning and running down the street.

"I'm on my way to my piano lesson at Mrs. Hershenson's house," Tori says. "She lives right there," pointing to the house on Beechwood Boulevard. "See you at India's game."

"Bye, Tori," I say.

"What about you, Sabeen?" Mom asks.

"Huh, what? Did someone say something to me?"

"Yes, I did. Would you like a ride home?"

"Oh, hi, Mrs. Champlin. I didn't see you there. No, thank you. I'm almost done reading my book. I want to time it so that when I get home, I'll be finished with it and then I can start a new one! Listen to this: 'String theory is about the nature of matter. It involves the existence of multiple parallel universes.' Do you know what that means?"

Our faces must look like big question marks, 'cause Sabeen doesn't even bother to wait for us to respond. Either that or she knows we're *totally* clueless and our silence is her answer.

"It means that people can occupy the same space at the same time. In other words, two people could stand and have a conversation in the same place that we are, and we wouldn't be able to see or hear them…nor they us. Isn't that fascinating?"

"Is that a rhetorical question?" I say under my breath. Don't know what it means, just know it sounds smart. Sabeen says it, and it seems like a great time to use it, even if no one hears me.

It's quiet. Does she really want us to answer her? Mom smiles at Sabeen while she stares google-eyed at her book as I hop into the car and put on my seatbelt.

"Okay, I'll bite," I say. "It does sound fascinating and scary at the same time. I mean, how do we know people are really there if we can't see or hear them? Are they ghosts?" Sabeen doesn't hear me; she's too busy reading. "Sabeen!" She still doesn't respond.

As we're about to drive off, I yell as loudly as I can, "Sabeen, watch your step!" She's about to walk into a pile of doggie uh-oh. Honestly, that girl. She knows *everything* about everything inside of books, but *nothing* about everything else. The girl has no common sense—at all. That's *one* thing she doesn't have that I've got a whole lot of.

The doggie uh-oh event gives me an idea. I'm gonna send an email message to our neighborhood secretary, Mrs. Willoughby, for her to remind people to clean up after their dogs!

On our way home I beg Mom to stop at the store to buy me some chewing gum. Something tells me this is going to be a looong weekend. And I need all the help I can get to help me stay focused and complete my writing assignment.

Here's what I write in my notebook Friday night:

My talents and special abilities
Friday night

• In third grade I helped Isaiah put the books back on the shelf in our classroom library after Real-to-Real made them fall off.

• I went to Tori Newman's piano recytle last year.

• I talk to my friends about eating healthy snacks.

• I help cheer my friends up when they're feeling sad.

• I obey the classroom rules.

• I hold the door open for my friends when we leave school.

• I went to the grosery store with mom and pushed the cart down the ille.

• I told mom and dad I loved them.

Chapter 5

Tweet

"Ahhhhh! Help! A chipmunk's in the house!"

A *what's* in the house? I turn the TV off and run into the kitchen. When I get there, Dee-O-Gee is going berserk, and Mom's on top of the kitchen table screaming half to death. There's a baby chipmunk scurrying around, trying to outrun Dee-O-Gee and skillfully dodging man-sized blows from the enormous broom clenched in Dad's hands.

"Arf, Arf..."

"How'd you get in here, you little rat?" Dad asks, swatting at the poor thing.

"Dad, it's a chipmunk, a *baby* chipmunk, not a rat."

"Arf, Arf, Arf, Arf..."

"Whatever it is, it's about to be..." he stops talking and swings at it instead. Good, he missed.

"Dad, it's just a chipmunk. Don't kill it."

"Yes, kill it, please kill it!" Mom screams at the top of her lungs.

"Arf, Arf, rrrrrrr." So does Dee-O-Gee.

"No! Let's capture it in the steel trap, take it to Frick Park, and let it go."

He takes another swing and looks at me. The chipmunk runs to a corner and doesn't move. Dad looks at the chipmunk then back at me.

"Okay. I'll make you a deal, September. If your plan doesn't work, if you can't capture it in the steel trap, that is, then we go to plan B."

"And plan B is...?"

"You know what plan B is, September." He leaves me with no other choice.

"Deal. I'll go get it."

I run as quickly as I can to the garage. *Now where is that trap?* I look everywhere: on top of the refrigerator, on boxes, shelves, through tons of ornaments and decorations, but no trap. I start to panic, thinking Dad killed it already, but that wasn't part of our deal. Come to think of it, it is awfully quiet in the house. Mom's not screaming, and Dee-O-Gee's not barking anymore. Oh no!

I turn to run back into the house and notice there's one place I didn't look, under a pile of old blankets on the floor covered in layers of dust, spider webs, and dirt. I run over to the blankets, snatch them up, cough, and toss them to the side. Nothing there. I run back into the house, coughing.

"Dad, I can't find..." I look on the floor and rub my eyes. The chipmunk is in the steel trap nibbling on a peanut.

"How did you...where'd you get the...?"

"After you went to the garage, I remembered I put it in the basement. There it was, plain as day," Dad says calmly. "No time to come and get you. Besides, we knew you'd come back soon."

"I was wondering why it was so quiet in the house."

"Yeah. I had to let Dee-O-Gee out because your mom was too afraid to get off the table." He turns to look at her and smiles, only she doesn't see him. Mom's sitting down with her forehead resting on the table, a bottle of aspirin next to her.

"Are you okay, Mom?" She doesn't answer me. "Mom, are you all right?" She mumbles something I don't understand; she stands, then walks down the hallway barefoot and goes upstairs.

"She'll be fine, September. You know how she feels about these things. Chipmunks are okay outside, but inside, that's a whole different story for her."

I shake my head.

We stare at the chipmunk still nibbling on the peanut. "Guess we caught the little fella before he had lunch," Dad says. We both chuckle.

"Can we let it go now? Pleeease," I ask as sweet as marshmallow sauce on top of vanilla ice cream.

Dad keeps his eyes on the chipmunk, wipes small drops of sweat off his nose with his long fingers, and leans against the counter.

"I'll tell you what, September, why don't you come with me today? I'm on my way to pick up Nathaniel to take him to our event at the Vintage Center. Before we get there, we'll let 'im go."

I don't like the sound of this. The Vintage Center is a place where old people go to do activities like yoga, painting, and dancing. Ever since Dad became a mentor in the Big Man Organization three years ago, he spends countless Saturday afternoons with Nathaniel, an eight-year-old boy who lives with his foster grandmother, Mrs. Jenkins, and two older sisters. He usually takes Nathaniel to places like the zoo, the Children's Museum, the Aviary, and the Science Center. Sometimes they'll even catch a movie or go to a hockey game.

"Nathaniel and the rest of the boys who signed up are supposed to bring books with them to read to the seniors in the center. Come with us. It'll be fun. There's gonna be a special guest listening while you read."

Did he say read? Ah, excuse me, today's Saturday. I don't read on the weekends.

"Who, the president?" I ask sarcastically.

"No, not the president, silly girl." Dad reaches to tickle me under my chin, but I pull away. He looks at me like he's reading my mind. He smiles and laughs as he speaks, "Oh, come on, September. You can put your feelings about reading aside for the time being. Besides, reading's not all that bad, you know. It's meant to be *enjoyed*! Notice how I emphasized the word *enjoyed*?" he asks, crossing his arms.

It's quiet. Dad's waiting for an answer.

"Oh, all right. I'll go. I'm not all that crazy about the idea, but I don't have anything better to do. All my friends are busy today."

"That's my girl!"

"Besides, I wanna make sure the chipmunk gets away safely. Plus it'll be good to see Nathaniel again. I haven't seen him in a while."

"We'll leave after I take a shower," Dad says, heading upstairs.

"Okay."

I cross my arms and wonder what I've gotten myself into. I uncross my arms, walk over to the refrigerator, and pour myself a glass of orange juice. *Well, at least I'll have something to write about in my notebook*, I think to myself. I take a few sips of orange juice, walk back to the steel trap, and bend down to look at the chipmunk. The peanut is completely gone. So is the chipmunk! I grab the trap and lift it up to make sure I'm seeing things clearly. Yep, it's gone. Oh, no! The latch is undone. *Where's the chipmunk? Is it still in the house, or did it run back outside?* Mom's resting and Dad's in the shower. I hear water running through the pipes. If I go now, I'll have plenty of time to trap another one and pretend it's the one Dad caught. That way he won't know the first one escaped. *But what if it's still in the house and Dee-O-Gee stumbles on it, or worse, Mom? Why not tell the truth?* If I tell the truth, Dad will probably spend the rest of the afternoon looking for it and he'll miss taking Nathaniel to the center. Nathaniel will be disappointed, no doubt. Dad will be down soon. I can't hear the water running anymore. I'd better start looking for it. I search the kitchen, top to bottom—the counters, the pantry, the cupboards. I even look behind the refrigerator. No signs of it anywhere. Then Dad walks in.

"Are you ready, September?" At the sound of his voice I stiffen and stand straight up the way a soldier stands at attention. My eyes are as big as Oreo cookies.

"I'm ready," I say, holding the trap behind me so he can't see the inside.

"You look like you've seen a ghost."

"I—I—I'm all right."

"You sure?"

"Ah-ha."

"Okey-dokey, let's go."

"Can we go to Frick Park first? I don't want the chipmunk to frighten Nathaniel."

"I hardly think a baby chipmunk locked in a cage will frighten an eight-year-old boy, but if you insist."

"Thanks, Dad."

On our way out, I finish my orange juice, then we let Dee-O-Gee back in the house. I grab Mom's new shirt and throw it over the trap so Dad doesn't notice it's empty.

"September, that's your mother's new shirt. Why'd you throw it over the trap?"

"Ahhh…because…chipmunks are nocturnal?" I think I give myself away when my voice goes up at the end of the word, "nocturnal." 'Course, I don't know if it's true or not, but it's all I can think of at the moment. Dad's looking at me funny.

"You don't say," he says, pulling at his whiskers. He's considering what I said, so I nod my head yes. "I knew bats and raccoons were nocturnal, but chipmunks?" he says, raising one eyebrow. "They're always scurrying around during the day." I don't know what to say, so I nod my head faster. "Then put an old towel or rag over it instead of your mother's new shirt. I don't want anything to happen to it. That way we'll both stay out of the doghouse."

"Yes, sir." Yes! Got outta that one. Guess I sounded more convincing than I looked. If that were Mom, she would have seen right through me.

I wait for Dad to walk out of the door before I exchange Mom's new shirt for an old rag. I grab my backpack, take out my Friday folder, and dump the rest of the peanuts in it so I can *pretend* to feed the *invisible* chipmunk on the way to a *real* park.

When we get there, I jump out of the car and run down the sidewalk. I yell back to Dad, "I'll do it myself. Be back in a minute."

"Okay," he says.

When I can't see Dad anymore, I count to ten then head back to the car. I put the trap in the trunk, then hop in the backseat and put on my seatbelt.

"We can go now."

"What did it do when you opened the latch?"

"He scurried away like a good little chipmunk."

"Good job, September. We make a good team, you and me."

I wish he hadn't said that. It makes me feel guilty. I feel terrible lying to Dad. But if I tell him the truth now, he'll be disappointed in me and he'd want to go back to the house to look for the chipmunk *and* check on Mom. Then he won't get to spend the afternoon with Nathaniel, something I know he's looking forward to. Maybe the chipmunk ran back outside the same way he came in the house. Then stayed out. If that's the case, I probably shouldn't say anything yet. Don't want to tell on myself for nothing.

Nathaniel's looking out of his living room window when we drive up to the house.

"Wait here, September. I'll be right back."

"Okay."

Looks like I won't be waiting long. Mrs. Jenkins brings him to the car. Nathaniel has his backpack with him. He gives her a hug, then gets in.

"Hi, Nathaniel."

"Hi, September."

We wave goodbye to Mrs. Jenkins as we take off for the center. After Nathaniel and I talk about our first week of school, he pulls out a book and reads until we get there. He reminds me of someone else I know. I'm quiet for the rest of the trip. I still feel bad about lying to Dad about the chipmunk cover-up and have decided to tell him the truth. But how and when?

We arrive at the Vintage Center and wait in the lobby for everyone else to come. When everybody has arrived, we're escorted to a large room at the end of the hallway. It smells like cleaning fluid in here. They probably use the room for banquets and parties. The room is very bright with lots of sunlight coming through the windows. Two of the walls in the room are covered with the seniors' paintings. There's a piano in a corner of the room, but it doesn't look like it gets much use. A cart with art supplies, paints, brushes, and tons of construction paper is next to the piano. On another wall there are three large bookcases. In front of them are tables of books. Sabeen would be in heaven right now. Comfortable-looking chairs and tables are set up around the room. Colorful child-sized rugs, like the kind in Mrs. Sullivan's kindergarten class, are placed next to each set of tables and chairs. About a dozen or so dog bowls filled with water are lined up against a wall, and small bags of dog treats are placed neatly on the windowsill. Huh? Dog bowls and dog treats?

"September. We're about to begin." Dad motions me over to the group.

"How ya'll doin'? Thanks for coming to visit with us this afternoon." Whoa, this man talks with the heaviest southern accent I've ever heard. *I wonder where he's from?*

"My name is Mr. Williams. I'm the director of the center. Your reading partners, that'll be the seniors, will be down in a few minutes. They're finishing up lunch. Our guests of honor, that'll be the dogs, will be here shortly, too."

So that's what's up with the dog bowls and dog treats. The dogs are the guests of honor. Cool.

"All the dogs participating in today's event are unique in some way. They've worked as dog guides, search and rescue dogs, or on the police force helping our law enforcement do everything from chasing down criminals to detecting harmful substances like narcotics and bombs. They're all well-trained older dogs who like the company of humans. By the way, if ya'll have any questions, feel free to ask, and, remember, there's no such thing as a dumb question."

"One time I was walking down the street and there was this horse. It was a small horse leading a woman. She was blind. The woman was blind, not the horse," a boy says.

"Man. You didn't see no horse leading a woman nowhere. Ain't no *guide horses*, boy."

"Yes I did!" the boy says with feeling.

"Where? I know you didn't see it down by *your* house."

"Okay, fellas, that's enough," Mr. Williams says. "Actually, there *are* guide horses. Some people who are visually impaired prefer them to dogs because they live longer."

Laughter explodes. The little boy who said he saw a guide horse looks at the other boy and makes a face at him. Only the boy doesn't see him do it. His face is buried in his hands 'cause he just got told.

"Amusement is over boys. Settle down, settle down," Mr. Williams says.

Nathaniel yells out, "Can I go to the bathroom?" *May I go to the bathroom?* I think to myself. I've been hanging around Sabeen too long.

"The door is right over there," Mr. Williams says. Nathaniel jumps up and runs to the bathroom.

"Any other questions or comments?" Another boy raises his hand.

"Yes, the young man in the blue and white striped shirt."

"Can I go to the bathroom, too?"

Maaay, I go to the bathroom? I think, again.

Mr. Williams chuckles to himself. "When he comes back, then you can go. Let me rephrase my question. Are there any questions pertaining to the dogs? Yes, the boy in the red shirt."

The little boy in the red shirt turns to his friends, watching them giggle. He frowns at them and tells them to stop giggling 'cause he was gonna ask "a real question this time." He looks back at Mr. Williams. "Are the dogs trained by veterinarians?"

A huge smile appears on Mr. Williams's face.

"Good question. No, actually a dog guide lives temporarily with an adoptive family when he or she is a puppy to be socialized around children. When the puppy reaches the age of one, it goes back to dog training school to continue to learn how to guide a person who's visually impaired. Search and rescue dogs, on the other hand, go to dog training schools and are taught by dog trainers."

Nathaniel rejoins the group, then the other boy runs over to the bathroom, holding his nose on the way in. More hands fly up in the air.

"Yes, you with the picture of a basketball player on his shirt."

"What happens when the police dogs get too old to work?"

"Most often the police take them home to live with them. They're rarely adopted into families."

While Mr. Williams continues to answer their questions, I walk over to the tables of books. My goal is to pick out short books, *really, really,* short books. I start thumbing through some, *Shiloh, The Slave Dancer, Julie of the Wolves,* and *Roll of Thunder, Hear My Cry.* No, these are chapter books. Why'd they include these? They'll take all day to read. I walk to another table of books. *Aunt Flossie's Hats (and Crab Cakes Later), Love You Forever, Abuela, Where the Wild Things Are, Dinner at Aunt Connie's House, Chicken Sunday, The Snowy Day.* This is more like it! Picture books are short and sweet.

I continue reading more titles like *Mufaro's Beautiful Daughters: An African Tale, Cloudy with a Chance of Meatballs, The Legend of the Bluebonnet, Jo Jo's Flying Sidekick.* There're so many, I don't know which ones to pick. They bring back memories of Mom and Dad reading to me when I was younger. I wouldn't say this out loud, but I actually like picture books. They're easy to read, and I like looking at the illustrations. That's why there's a stack of 'em on my bedroom floor.

"All right. Thanks for ya'll's questions. Well, lookie here, our guests of honor have arrived."

The dogs are brought in by their owners and gather around Mr. Williams. There are golden retrievers, Labrador retrievers, German shepherds, border collies, bloodhounds, and beagles. I stop what I'm doing and walk toward the dogs and so does everyone else.

Mr. Williams announces, "While we're still waiting for the seniors to come, I'd like to take this opportunity to once again thank everyone for coming out this fine afternoon. I have a feeling we're all in for a very special treat." Mr. Williams stops, looks at the door, and then checks his watch. "Since the seniors still haven't arrived, let's go ahead and have the children get better acquainted with their guest of honor." The boys get excited and start cheering. "If I can have the owners of the dogs find a spot on one of the carpets."

The owners follow his instructions, guiding the dogs through a maze of tables and chairs. Mr. Williams waits patiently until everyone finds a spot.

"Wonderful. Now let's have the adults help these fine young gentlemen..." He stops. He dips his head toward me and says, "and lady find a dog they'd be comfortable reading with this afternoon."

I smile at him.

The boys quickly scramble throughout the room while the dogs remain remarkably calm.

Nathaniel runs toward a German shepherd. When he reaches it, he holds out his hand. The dog slobbers it up. Dad's next to him, gently stroking the dog. I spot a golden retriever and walk over to it.

"What's its name?" I say to the owner.

"Her name's Symphony."

"That's a cute name."

"Yeah," the owner says back.

"What'd she do that was so special?"

"She was a dog guide."

"She was?"

"Ah-ha."

"Why'd she stop?"

"She became blind."

"She's blind?" His response surprises me. She doesn't look blind.

"Yeah. She is."

"How'd she go blind?"

"She had a disease that caused her to lose her eyesight."

I turn and stare into Symphony's eyes. "What's the name of the disease?"

"Glaucoma."

I wave my hand in front of her, and then move it to the left, then to the right, and back to the left again. She didn't follow my hand. I touch her nose gently; it's cold and wet.

"What's glaucoma?" I ask.

"When there's too much pressure in the eye." He pauses. "Did you notice how she tilted her head to the side when you waved your hand in front of her face?"

"Ah-ha."

"That's her way of *seeing* you," he says, raising his eyebrows while gesturing quotation marks around the word seeing.

"Oh, cool."

"Would you like me to stay with you when you read with your

partner?"

"No, I'll be fine. I'm used to dogs. I have a dog at home, a Yorkie, named Dee-O-Gee."

He smiles, nods, and then hands me her leash. "She's very well-behaved."

"All right."

"Perfect timing," Mr. Williams announces. "Look who the wind blew in!"

The seniors! They're *reeeally* old, but they look so happy to see us and the dogs. They start walking and shuffling our way; some are pushed in wheelchairs.

I'm so busy petting Symphony I almost don't even notice a small, frail man with wrinkled skin a deep brown color standing in front of me.

"Hello, there," he says. "Name's Tweet."

Tweet? That's a funny name.

"Hi. I'm September and this is Symphony. She's blind."

"Pleasure," he says, patting Symphony on the head.

Tweet's wearing an old black suit, a dingy white shirt, although it might be gray, I can't tell, and a tattered black hat. He looks a hot mess, but he doesn't smell, so I don't mind being close to him. He walks with a reddish brown cane with carvings on it. He shuffles to the chair and plops down, almost missing it.

I glance at Nathaniel already reading. His dog is resting on his leg and his reading partner is sound asleep. The adults are scattered around the room talking with each other and helping the boys pick out other books to read. Dad keeps a close eye on Nathaniel and checks on me as well.

I look up at Tweet, trying my best to do the right thing and look past his clothes 'cause Grandma Lipscomb taught me clothes don't make a person. "Is there a certain book you'd like me to read?" I hesitate. I've never called an adult by their first name before, only to myself when I called Mrs. Bridgewaters Odessa. "Tweet." He's silent for a moment.

"Whatever you read is fine with me," he says with a shaky voice.

"Okay, the first book I'm going to read is called *When I Am Old with You*, by Angela Johnson and illustrated by David Soman. I chose it because I like the cover."

I open the book and begin reading, showing the pictures to Tweet after I read the page. All his oohing and aahing reminds me of reading with the five-year-olds in Mrs. Sullivan's kindergarten class.

I read half a dozen or so more books and then ask Tweet if he'd like to read. He looks at me with sadness in his eyes.

"I don't know how to read."

I slowly turn my head away from Tweet. There's a part of me that doesn't want to look at him; I'm embarrassed by his confession. What he said reminds me of myself and how much I don't like to read.

"Wah, what'd you say?" I ask, looking at the seniors' artwork on the wall. *Wow! There're some beautiful pictures up there.*

Tweet doesn't respond. *Have I hurt his feelings?* Out of guilt, I slowly look back at him. He's looking down at Symphony licking her front paw. When he looks at me, his words aren't more than a whisper. "I don't know how to read," he repeats. He doesn't appear to be embarrassed at all by his confession…just sad. I'm both.

Leaning back in his chair, he takes his hat off his shiny bald head and gently places it on his skinny knee, but it slips off. He carefully puts it on the table instead. Then he rests his hands on top of his cane directly out in front of him. If I didn't know any better, I'd a thought he was getting ready to preach a sermon or something.

"I was born in 1920 in Dothan, Alabama, a few years after World War I ended, the oldest of six children. Daddy was a farmer. Farmed pecan trees, acres and acres of pecan trees. Mama had her hands full with the little ones. Never had time for school, too busy helpin' Daddy plant, grow, tend to the trees. Went my whole life, *eighty-one years,*" he stops, tears swell in his eyes, "without learnin' how to read. They say I read like a first grader." He looks at me. "Darlin', can you imagine what it's like livin' your *entire life* without knowin' how to read?" He pauses and looks upward, like he's looking at something or someone. "I can sign my own name, though. Yeees, Lawd. I can sign my own name." He wipes the tears from his eyes. Symphony raises her head, sniffs the air around her like she's reading the room, and then she gently lowers it.

"Would you like to learn how to read someday, if you don't mind me asking?" I question him, stroking Symphony on her back.

Tweet starts laughing and says loudly, which I didn't know he could, "You can't…you can't teach an old dog new tricks!"

The room grows quiet as his words fill in around us. Everyone's staring at us. Symphony raises her head again, tilts it to the side, and gives a low, steady growl.

"Easy girl," I whisper, continuing to stroke her back.

Seconds go by, the muffled sound of voices picks up again. Tweet starts coughing, then stops.

"Too late to learn now. I was sent up north to Pittsburgh to live with Uncle Zeek and his wife, Auntie Mae, when Daddy lost the farm during the Great Depression. I was nine years old. Just too many mouths to feed, I guess. Never went to school when I got to Pittsburgh, started workin'. When I turned thirteen, I got me a job down by the railroad tracks in the Strip District unloadin' produce and fresh meat into warehouses and grocery stores. Didn't need to know how to read unloadin' stuff." He turns and looks down at Symphony and says quietly, "Just strong arms." He sighs. "And a strong back."

He looks at his wrinkled hands still resting on his cane, then looks out the window into the sunshine. His voice is weak when he speaks again. "Never had me a driver's license. Never read the newspaper. Never read from a menu. Why, I've never even been in a public library. No need to, if you can't read."

I'm saddened by his honesty.

He lifts those bushy eyebrows when he looks at me, long and steady.

"Do you like to read?" His question catches me off guard.

"Wah, what'd you ask me?"

"I didn't stutter."

I know he didn't stutter. I heard him perfectly well, but I've already lied to Dad about the chipmunk; I don't want to lie to Tweet, too.

"I said, do you like to read?" he asks again, then he places his cane across his lap, a half-smile is on his face.

"Uh-huh, I like to read," I say, petting Symphony on the head. What I told him was true; I do like to read—picture books—at least I did up to an hour ago.

Me and Tweet talk for the rest of the afternoon. The more he talks, the more I realize his life was like a storybook: one exciting adventure after another.

"I hopped on one of them there boxcars from Pittsburgh back to Alabama to visit my kinfolk, then hitchhiked back to Pittsburgh. I floated on a raft I made from some old tree logs and twine down the Missouri River once, too." He pauses and rubs his hand on that shiny bald head of his, laughing to himself.

Even the carvings he made on his cane represent people from his past.

"The stars are my brothers and sisters, and the sun and moon Mama and Daddy."

He said no matter where he goes he always senses their presence. He didn't say it like that, but I knew what he meant.

Tweet even told me how he got his nickname.

"My real name is Jeffery Tod Mandu Jones II. It's a mouthful, I know."

Tweet bursts out laughing, then slaps his knee. His cane almost falls off his lap, but he catches it.

"One day when I was about eleven, I went duck hunting with Uncle Zeek. I studied the sounds the ducks made and repeated them to Uncle. Old Uncle Zeek was so impressed in my *special ability*, as he called it, to call them ducks, he took me every time he went duck hunting. When I called 'em, the poor things came flying right into the open arms of Uncle Zeek. Wasn't long before I learned how to make all kinds of birdcalls and was given the name Tweet by Uncle. Wanna know somethin'?"

I nod like I'm super happy.

"Some of the happiest days of my life were spent walking in the woods whistling with the birds. Listen carefully to the birds now. You may think they sound the same from day to day, but they don't sound the same at all. No sirree. Their sounds are as different and unique as we are. Everyday they sing a new song. Think of me when you hear them. I'll be thinkin' of you, too."

Tweet turns and stares out the window. Then he starts whistling. After a while, I start humming along the way I do when I forget the words to a song.

Dad puts a hand on my shoulder. "Time to go, September."

"Already?"

I look around. The room is slowly clearing out. I was having so much fun talking with Tweet, I didn't realize it was time to go home. Symphony's owner walks over. We say our goodbyes and then he leads her to water and treats. I say goodbye to Tweet, but don't move to leave.

I bend down to give him a hug and whisper in his ear, "Thanks, Tweet. I'd like to come back and read with you again."

He looks up at me and says, "That'd be mighty nice. Yes siree, that'd be mighty nice, indeed." Then he throws me a whistle.

It's quiet on our drive home. Nathaniel's sleeping, and I'm looking out the window, thinking about my day with Tweet. For someone who can't read, I'm amazed by the way he tells stories similar to the ones we read today. But for all the exciting stories he told about his life, I can't shake feeling sorry for him 'cause he can't read. He's never read a newspaper. He's never even been in a public library, for goodness' sake. I don't like to read, but at least I know *how* to. *I wonder what'll happen to me if I stop reading altogether? Will I end up at the Vintage Center, sad and pitiful like Tweet? What will I miss out on if I don't become a book reader? What have I missed out on already?*

I turn and catch sight of Dad's eyes from the rearview mirror. He glances at me and smiles. I know what his smile means. I'm glad I came, too. I look away, trying to give myself time to tell him about the chipmunk cover-up. Then I change my mind. I reach into the side pocket of my backpack and stick a piece of gum in my mouth instead.

Nathaniel's still sleeping when we drive up to his house. He's so tired he doesn't even budge when I unbuckle his seatbelt. Dad reaches to lift him into his arms.

"He's one tired little dude," he says with affection in his voice.
I smile at Dad as I hand him Nathaniel's backpack.

While I watch Dad carry Nathaniel up to the house, I start thinking about what I'll record in my notebook tonight.

Here's what I write before I go to bed:

My talents and best qualities
Saturday night

- I helped dad catch a chipmunk in our house, but it got away.

- I went to the Vintage Center and read stories all afternoon with Tweet and Symphoney.

- I listened to Tweet tell lots of stories about his life.

- Once I put some money in an envelope and asked my mom to give it to the poor.

- I clean my room without being asked to clean it.

- I try to always remember to say thank you and to compliment people.

- I told mom and dad I loved them.

Chapter 6

Plain, Stripes, or Polka Dots

I try to pay attention to Pastor Farmer's sermons, but my mind starts to wander and I start thinking about all the things I have to do after church.

"Have mercy," Dad responds to the pastor.

I write them down so I won't forget. It also keeps me from falling asleep. Mr. Outlaw should try it sometime. He always falls asleep right before they collect the offering.

Things to do after church today:

- Eat lunch

- Email Mrs. Willowbee about doggie uh-oh

- Go to India's soccer tournament

- Tell mom and dad about chipmunk cover-up

- Write in notebook

45

"Can—I—GET—a witness?" the pastor asks the congregation.

"Hallelujah," the congregation responds.

I like going to church. Been at Bethany Baptist my whole life. It's the one place, other than my bedroom, that I feel totally safe.

"Aaaa-men!" Mom responds.

"Heh-choo."

"Ooh, gross! Right on my hands. Makayla, why didn't you cover?"

"Sorry, September. I didn't mean to sneeze on…"

Mom places a finger to her lips. "Shhhhh. Here, September. Wipe your hands on this tissue," she says softly.

I take the tissue from Mom and wipe in between every one of my fingers. I think it was too late, though. Sabeen says it takes about as long as it takes to sing the *Happy Birthday* song twice for germs to spread on our body. Makayla's germs were there ten, twenty, a zillion minutes before I wiped them off. I'm not sitting next to her next week…seriously!

"Moving on in our service, after a selection from the children's choir, my message this morning will come from the book of Ephesians, chapter 4, verse 32. 'Be kind to one another, tender-hearted, forgiving one another as God has forgiven you.' The title of my sermon is *Forgiveness: What's Forgetting Have to Do with It?*"

No response. Complete silence.

"Heh-choo."

"Makayla!!"

"Pastor Farmer and his wife are planning to adopt another child," Mom says before she takes a bite of her sandwich.

"That's nice."

"Sure was a good sermon he preached today, wasn't it?" she asks with food in her mouth.

"Ah-ha," I say slowly, *except for getting sneezed on,* I think as I tap my spoon against the side of my bowl. I'm sad. Dad's busy packing for a business trip. He's a financial planner and has a meeting in New York City. His meeting isn't until Tuesday, but he wants to get there early so he can do some sightseeing. After the meeting, he's going to his Aunt Lucinda's house in Brooklyn. He's going to paint her kitchen purple—she wants it purple!

"ROSE-MAR-EEE, HAVE YOU SEEN MY BLACK SOCKS WITH THE GOLD TOE?" Dad shouts.

"THEY'RE IN YOUR TOP DRAWER. I JUST WASHED THEM," Mom yells back. There's a pause.

"I FOUND THEM. THANK YOU."

"YOU'RE WELCOME, SAGE."

"I heard that."

Dad's voice trails off. Mom chuckles. His first name is Robert, not Sage. She likes teasing him—her name being Rosemary and all. She smiles, looks down at her sandwich, shakes her head, and mumbles something to herself. I know what that means—why doesn't he look first? Dad doesn't bother looking because he knows Mom knows where everything is. By asking first, it's his way of saving time looking for things.

Dad walks into the kitchen with his suitcase.

"Ladies, what looks better, plain, stripes, or polka dots?"

Mom and I look at each other and say at the same time, "Definitely plain." Dad stuffs the plain tie in his suitcase.

"Did you pack your painting gear?" Mom asks.

"Yep."

"Oh, don't forget your inhaler."

"I've got it right here," he says, patting his pants pocket. He's had asthma ever since he was a child. He had a severe attack when he was in high school playing football and was rushed to the hospital because he left his inhaler at home. He said he learned his lesson and will never forget it again. But I've noticed Mom has to remind him to take it every once in a while.

"All right, I think I'm ready."

I get up from my chair and give him a big squeeze.

"Goodbye, Daddy. I love you."

"I love you, too, my little angel. Help your mom around the house while I'm gone."

"I will."

"When I get back, the two of us will go somewhere special."

"Like where?"

"I don't know, but it'll be special!"

"I can't wait for you to come back."

I know it sounds selfish of me, but inside I'm secretly hoping Aunt Lucinda will change her mind about him painting her kitchen purple just so he can come back sooner and take me to that special place.

Dad gives me a kiss and then grabs his suitcase. Now's probably not a good time to tell him about the chipmunk cover-up. I'll tell him later. The three of us walk Dad to the car. It's gotten a lot windier since we went to church. I turn my head away from Mom and Dad to give them some privacy while they kiss. *One Mississippi—Two Mississippi—Three Mississippi—Four Mississippi.* Wow! That was a long kiss. When they finish, Dad pats Dee-O-Gee on the head and says, "Be a good dog." Dee-O-Gee wags his tail and looks at him as if he understands. You know, sometimes I think he does.

It takes Dad fifteen seconds to back out of the driveway. It normally takes ten, but the wind knocked the garbage can down and Mom has to move it. We follow his car down the street until it's out of sight. When we walk back into the house, Dee-O-Gee lays down on his pillow in the family room, and Mom grabs the laundry from the dryer and starts singing some old Michael Jackson song—something about making the world a better place to live in.

I try to keep a straight face, but I don't want to be ornery. Let's see…what's the name of that song? Ohhh, it's on the tip of my tongue, but I can't remember it. Mom dances *her* version of hip-hop into the kitchen, holding a laundry basket, still singing the song.

"They're calling for rain this afternoon." She puts the basket on the table.

I'm in full-blown laughter. I can't help myself. There's just something about watching my mother try to dance like a seventeen-year-old that makes a girl forget that her father just left on a business trip to New York City and won't return until he paints his aunt's kitchen purple. Mom always knows how to cheer me up.

"I know," I say, laughing. "I'll take my raincoat and umbrella to the game.

  la, la, la,

  la, la, la…"

"Do you have any homework this weekend?" she asks folding a towel.

  "Hoo, hoo, hoo…"

"Yes. Sort of.

  Hoo, hoo…"

"What do you mean by that, 'sort of?'" Mom asks.

"Well, I'm the only one Mrs. Bridgewaters gave homework to this weekend."

"Why are *you* the only one?"

"Because I was having a hard time coming up with ideas to write about," I reply.

"What kind of ideas?"

"We have to write about our talents or best qualities, but I couldn't think of anything to write about. She told me to jot down all the nice things I've done for people in the past and to write down everything I do this weekend as a way to come up with some ideas to write about."

"Do you have to write about everything you do?"

"Everything I can remember. I write at night before I go to bed. Like when I went to the Vintage Center and read with Tweet, I put that down yesterday."

"Did you email Mrs. Willoughby yet?" Mom asks.

"Not yet. But I will."

"After you email her, you can write that down, too."

"Okay."

Mom folds another towel and sings, *"Make a change."*

Both of us are in full-blown laughter. We bow toward each other and then fold the rest of the towels.

We sing songs and fold laundry for so long that I lose track of time. Before Mom drives me to India's soccer tournament, she helps me send an email message to Mrs. Willoughby about the doggie uh-oh.

Chapter 7

Gifted Math

I've always wanted to touch a cloud, but today is the exception. The sky has turned to the color of mud. The sudden gusts of wind have increased; it even smells like it's going to rain. But none of these things has stopped people from coming to the tournament. There are lots of people here. Sabeen and Tori are sitting on the sideline away from the crowds. Sabeen's reading a book…wait, no, I'm wrong. I can't believe my eyes. What in heaven's name? I'm about to jump through my skin. Sabeen brought her kitten instead of a book! She also got her hair cut.

"Hey, you two, or should I say three?"

"Bonjour mes amis," Sabeen says.

"Hay is for cows," says Tori, pretending to play the piano in the air.

"Whatever, Tori." I see she has an attitude today so I turn my attention to Sabeen.

"Sabeen, I like your hair."

"Merci."

"Turn around. Let me see the back."

She throws her head to the side like a model. We all start laughing. A gust of wind blows her hair in her face. Sabeen shakes her head back and pushes her hair behind her ear.

"She cut off a little too much, but I still like it."

My hair's way thicker and way curlier than Sabeen's. And right now, way longer. I mostly wear it in a ponytail.

"And who do we have here?" I say stroking her kitten's back. "Stop. Before you answer that, where's your book?"

"My mom wouldn't let me bring one because she didn't think I could hold a book and Balzac at the same time."

I watch her rub his tiny head and then *zoing,* it hit me. She said she named him Balzac! Balzac? I even try to spell *B-a-l-l-z-a-c* several times in my head before I open my mouth 'cause Grandma Lispcomb and Mom taught me to think before I speak.

"Balzac? No offense, but why'd you name him Balzac? Whatever happened to names like Whiskers, Deuce, Cuddles, Mr. Gigglesworth, or…?"

"Mr. Gigglesworth? Who was he? Was he famous?" Sabeen asks eagerly.

"Calm down, Sabeen," I say motioning for her to relax. "No. It's just a cute cat name."

"Oh. Well, Balzac was a famous French writer of the nineteenth century and a voracious reader, like me."

Here she goes again. I hate when she talks about French stuff. Since I don't understand what she's saying, I turn my attention to the soccer field just in time to watch India score her team's first goal of the game.

"Way to go, India!" I shout. I was the only one to see her score.

Tori's still pretending to play the piano, and Sabeen's *still* talking to me—at me is more like it.

"I've read all of his literary works in French and in English. I love his writing style. That's why I named him Balzac," Sabeen says in her spelling-bee-contest-winner voice.

"That's nice," I say, not understanding a word of it. Tori suddenly stops playing the piano.

"Hey, I have a great idea. Why not make his middle name Mr. Gigglesworth?" she asks, jokingly.

September's Big Assignment

Me and Tori start giggling. I think it's a purrfect idea, but Sabeen doesn't think it's funny. While giggling, I notice Tori's wobbly tooth.

"Tori, you still haven't lost your tooth!"

"What? Oh, nope. I thought it would come out yesterday when I bit into my apple dipped in honey, but it didn't."

"When you bit…that's why I wanted to trade my apple for your chocolate pudding at lunch on Friday. So your tooth would come out!"

"I know, September. I didn't want to trade because I didn't want to accidently swallow it."

"What?"

"That happened to my sister, Lizzie. She swallowed her tooth at school when she was eating lunch."

"What happened to it?" I say.

"What happened to *her* or *it?*"

Let me think this through. *If I ask what happened to Lizzie, Tori may get jealous. On the other hand, if I ask what happened to her tooth she might think I don't care about Lizzie. Should I drop the topic, or should I ask about Lizzie? What's the worst that can happen? Tori de-friend me, stop speaking to me for a day, a week, or month?* I've made a decision.

I decide to say, "Both."

"She was fine."

Her response surprises me, no visual signs of jealously, no drama. Tori's finally growing up! Or has she forgotten she's supposed to be jealous?

"What do you *think* happened to it?" Tori says, looking at me like she has to spell it out.

"How should I know," I ask. "I wasn't there…when…oooooh, now I get it."

"All right, all right, you two," Sabeen says, sounding all grown-up, as usual. She glances at both of us like she's bored with our conversation. "Can we change the subject?"

"Fine by me," Tori replies. I'm ready to move on, too.

"Can I hold him? I mean, *may* I hold him?"

She looks at me out of the corner of her eyes. *What?* I corrected

53

myself. She twists her lips. *Now what?*

She cracks a smile and says, "Yes!" He's curled up in a fluff ball when she hands him to me.

"He's sooo soft." He sure looks like a Mr. Gigglesworth to me. While rubbing his belly, I notice the clouds turned muddier in color.

"Who's winning?" Tori asks.

"India's team," I say. "The score's one, no, two to nothing." India just scored again.

"Go, India!" we shout.

India's running up the field like she has wheels on her feet. Her hair is blowing every direction in the wind. A gazelle. That's what she looks like, a gazelle, wearing a green headband and a pair of matching shin pads. She's so fast her teammates can't even catch up to her to celebrate with her. They're running around all wacky, like a bunch of kittens playing with a ball of string.

Suddenly, I feel raindrops on my head.

"Uh-oh, it's starting to rain." We open our umbrellas.

Sabeen immediately calls her mom.

"Mom, it's starting to drizzle. Can you pick us up? He's dry right now, but I don't want him to get wet. Ah-ha, okay. We'll be ready. My mom has a quick errand to run, then she'll swing by and pick us up. We'll drop you off at your house, September, after we take Tori to her piano lesson. You'll be a little early today, Tori."

"That's okay. I hope she comes soon. I don't want my piano books to get wet."

"Sit on them," I reply.

"Brilliant idea. Why didn't I think of that?"

I roll my eyes at her.

"Listen," I say.

"Listen to what?" says Tori.

"To Balzac. He's purring. I love hearing that sound. It's soothing, like the smell of lavender."

"I haven't been able to make him do that yet," Sabeen says. "What'd you do?"

"I didn't do anything. I'm just gentle with him, that's all."

Soon there's a steady drizzle.

"I don't want Balzac to get wet," Sabeen says.

"Let's wrap him in my raincoat while you hold the umbrella over him," I say.

"Okay."

The rain picks up to a stronger drizzle. I'm getting chilly. I look at the scoreboard, still two to nothing. India looks our way and gives a friendly wave. We wave back.

"Look. Now India's giving us the peace sign," I say.

"No, she's telling us she scored two points. That's a no-brainer, September," Tori replies.

"How do you know it's not the peace sign?" I argue, knowing perfectly well that what she said could be true. Still, what I said could be true, too.

"Because I'm good in math, and it's obvious she's letting us know she scored two points for her team. Furthermore, if that were *me*, I'd want people to know *I* scored two points," she snaps.

"Take it down an octave, Tori. I'm sitting right next to you. And, oh yeah, I say it's the peace sign."

"I say it's two points."

"Peace sign." I don't know why I'm friends with Tori. Sometimes I think the only thing we have in common is our curly hair.

"Two points," she says.

"Peace…sign!"

"Two…points." Tori sounds angry. "If you couldn't tell that India held up two fingers, for two points, quite frankly, September, then that's your problem."

"Doggonit, Tori! You don't know everything!"

"I know I'm in gifted math," Tori says confidently, very sure of herself.

What follows is a painful, awkward silence; I'm not sure what to say next. I'm thinking this is a friendly argument, but from the looks of things, Tori doesn't. There's no warmth on her face; she's looking at me with icicles in her eyes. Her look seems to draw out the worst in me. Suddenly I feel like I'm going to lose control. A knot of anger swells in my throat and my hand balls into a fist. From the back of my mind Pastor Farmer's words come and settle in the front of my brain: *Turn the other cheek. Take the high road.* I think about this for a nanosecond. Guess what? Pastor Farmer has his way of fighting battles, and I have mine. My eyes narrow at Tori and hers at mine. She hasn't blinked in the last two minutes. A goofy smile slowly covers her face. Her lips part. She breaks the silence between us, one word at a time. Her voice is cold. "I'm—in—gifted—mah…"

From out of nowhere a gust of wind throws me backward and Tori never finishes her sentence. She doesn't have to; I know what she's going to say. The screaming and hollering are all a blur. Then there's the high-pitched, shrill sound the soccer ball makes—wheeeeee and bam—a direct hit to her mouth. Tori takes a blow to the face with the soccer ball. The ball hits her so hard she falls to the ground, backward, and blood oozes uncontrollably from her mouth and nose.

She immediately starts crying and holds her hands over her mouth, blood splattering through her fingers and going everywhere, mixing with the rain on her clothes, shoes, piano books… oh, Tori's piano books! I grab them and clutch them tightly in my arms. I can't say why, only that I'm torn between reaching out and helping Tori and watching her suffer all at the same time. Sabeen's already on her phone calling Tori's mom.

I'm in shock and scared from the sight of all the blood. Inside, I smile a secret smile to myself—that oughta teach her a lesson to stop bragging about her special abilities. *I'm in gifted math, I'm in gifted math.* Who cares if you're in gifted math and you can't even see a soccer ball coming twenty miles an hour at you, heading straight toward your face! Look where it got you—on the ground with blood gushing out of your brains! Hey, Tori, how fast does a soccer ball need to travel in order to hit its target spot-on? Twenty miles an hour? Get it? How gifted are you now, eh? Toughen up, buttercup.

"Tori, are you okay?" Sabeen asks nervously several times before everyone, including both soccer teams, rush over to us.

Tori doesn't respond. She's in too much pain. About all she can do is cry, roll on the wet ground, and cover her mouth with her hands.

"Poor Tori," Sabeen says, looking at me and then Tori.

I try to keep the umbrella over her head, but say nothing. I'm still angry over what she said and was *about* to say. The team paramedic, nearly out of breath, reaches Tori first.

"What's your friend's name?" she asks, huffing and puffing.

"Tori," I answer.

"Tori," she gulps, putting her stubby fingers with chipped red nail polish on Tori's shoulders. "My name is Mrs. Shapiro. I'm an emergency paramedic." Tori's literally crying her head off. "I need you to lay still and put your hands down so I can examine you. Can you do that for me, honey?"

Tori nods, still crying her head off.

"Good. Poor little girl," Mrs. Shapiro says, then shouts over her shoulder, "Give the poor girl some room please, people!" She motions the crowd to step back, including Sabeen.

"Is she going to be okay?" India asks like she's apologizing, taking short steps backward away from us.

"She's going to be fine," her coach tells her. "Let's take a timeout break."

India walks back to the bench with her coach like they're in a secret discussion about something. I can imagine how India feels right now: guilty, like she'll owe Tori something for the rest of her life. It was India that kicked the soccer ball that hit Tori in the face. I saw the players coming closer and closer to us out of the corner of my eye when we were arguing. I couldn't tear my eyes away to warn her, then the gust of wind came and…Everything happened so fast.

I start walking with the crowd when Mrs. Shapiro looks at me, "Not youuu…" she holds on to the word "you" waiting for me to say my name.

"September."

"September?" She looks surprised, like she's never heard of someone named September before.

"September, I want you to stay with your friend. Keep the umbrella over her face while I take care of her, will ya honey?"

"Sure," I say, squatting next to Tori.

Watching Tori cry draws me toward her, and a wave of guilt hits me and knocks me off my feet, and brings me to my senses. *What was I thinking allowing anger to take control of my feelings toward my friend like that?* I wish I could take those words and thoughts back, but I can't. They came and went, like the surge of wind that whirled the soccer ball into Tori's face in the first place. Truth is, Tori's comfortable being Tori. She doesn't look down on herself like I do. She's confident, and there's a part of me that's jealous of that. In fact, deep down inside me, there's a part of me that wants nothing more than to be just like Tori, the strong and confident part, that is. 'Cause in many ways, Tori's everything I'm not.

"Keep the umbrella steady, October."

"It's September."

"I'm sorry, September, honey."

"That's okay. I'm used to it."

Tori's no longer crying, but lets out a soft whimper every now and then. Mrs. Shapiro gently dabs and wipes her gashes and cleans all the dirt the soccer ball and Tori's dirty hands left behind.

"Will she need stitches?"

"Surprisingly, no."

Tori and I don't speak to each other as the rain continues to pound down on the umbrella. After nearly fifteen minutes of careful attention, Mrs. Shapiro finishes and says, "I think that about does it."

Tori struggles to sit up. I grab hold of her arm and gently pull her forward.

"Is someone coming to take her home?" She hesitates then looks at me like she's searching for a forgotten thought, "November."

"It's Sep-tem-ber. September."

"Sorry, September. I knew it was the name of a month. I just couldn't remember which one."

"Her mother's coming. She'll be here shortly."

"Keep these ice packs on your face. Okay, honey?" Tori nods and takes the ice packs from her as she tries to smile a thank you.

"I couldn't have done this without your help, October," Mrs. Shapiro says.

What's the use in correcting her? I don't get why she can't remember my name. It's not even hard to pronounce.

I sigh and say, "You're welcome."

Mrs. Shapiro smiles at Tori, pats her on the shoulder with those stubby fingers and chipped red nail polish, then walks back to the team bench without an umbrella to cover her.

Tori looks cautiously at me, and then she gives a weak, crooked smile. Her eyes are puffy and red. The icicles in her eyes have melted.

"Well, how do I look...November?" she asks, sounding like she stuffed a handful of cotton balls in her mouth.

I smile at her, not because I'm happy she got hurt, but because I feel toasty inside, like I feel when Mom has a plateful of warm chocolate chip cookies waiting for me when I come home from school.

"Like a million bucks."

My response makes Tori smile a little straighter, even through swollen, bee-stung lips and bruises on her face, which is covered by large bandages on her nose that stretch from one side of her face to the other. Though neither one of us says it, I can tell by the look in her eyes that she's sorry for the things she said. Me too.

While smiling, I notice something astonishing: she lost her tooth, not her wobbly tooth, her permanent, adult, grown-up tooth. A tooth that was once rock solid in her mouth is now busted out from a blow to her face with a soccer ball, and the wobbly tooth is still wobbly. *How can that be?* I think, as my heart reaches out to Tori. I give her a big hug and then she leans her head on me.

"Tori," I say in a voice that's almost a whisper.

"Yes," she replies quietly.

"Where's your tooth? Did Mrs. Shapiro give it to you?"

Tori doesn't respond right away. She feels the gap in her tooth with her tongue.

"I swallowed it," she says considerately. Tori leans forward and stares right into my eyes.

Sabeen appears with Balzac nestled in her arms, still covered in my raincoat. She glances at me then bends down to give Tori a big hug. Balzac's in the middle and gets squished. I search for words to comfort Tori while we wait for her mother in the rain, but nothing comes. I start singing a bunch of Michael Jackson songs. Sabeen joins in. After a while, my mind starts drifting. Without even realizing it, I start thinking about Tweet and my songs become a soft hum.

I never saw that goofy smile on Tori's face ever again.

The smell of furniture polish hits me when I walk through the front door.

"Mom, guess what?"

"Hi, September. Did they cancel the game because of the rain?" Mom asks while wiping the dining room table.

"No. They didn't, but they could've. We didn't stay for the whole game," I say quickly. I kick my shoes off and toss them by the front door. "Guess what?"

"I'm glad you didn't stay the whole time." She walks into the kitchen and puts the polish underneath the sink.

I follow her, saying, "Mrs. Merriweather picked us up. She showed up right after Mrs. Neuman came."

"Oh. That was nice of her."

"Mom, I have something to tell you! Are you *ever* going to *answer* me?" I ask impatiently.

"Now wait just a minute, September!" Mom says back like I hurt her feelings.

"Sorry, Mom."

"I know, that's right."

"But I've been trying to tell you something ever since I got home. You're not listening to me."

"Well, now that you have my undivided attention, what would you like to tell me?"

"There was an accident at India's game today."

Her face looks worried.

"There was? What happened?"

"India kicked the soccer ball and hit Tori in the mouth and knocked out a permanent tooth!"

Mom gasps. "Oh no! Poor Tori. Is she okay? Did she need stitch-es?"

"Yes, she's okay and no, she didn't need stitches."

Mom looks relieved.

"We were on the sideline arguing...I mean talking and the next thing I knew Tori was lying on the ground bleeding like crazy. The ball hit her straight in the mouth and knocked it right out. Here's the strange part: her wobbly tooth didn't get knocked out, but her permanent tooth did. Isn't that weird?"

Mom is looking at me very seriously. "Yes, that is."

"Mrs. Shapiro, India's team paramedic, took care of her, with my assistance."

"With your assistance? What did you do?"

"I held the umbrella over Tori's face so she didn't get wet. Mrs. Shapiro kept calling me October or November. She never got my name right."

Mom nods, but doesn't smile. "We should probably check on Tori a little later on."

I toss my raincoat over a kitchen chair. Mom stares at my coat, then at me.

She's quiet a moment, then looks at my coat again. "September, if I've told you once, I've told you a thousand times, hang—your—coat—up!"

"Yes, ma'am." I walk to the hall closet and hang my coat on a hook. I walk back into the kitchen.

"Now what's this about you arguing with Tori?"

"It's no big deal, really. We made up."

"What were you arguing about?"

"To make a long story short, Tori thinks she knows everything. The argument was about a disagreement we had. She saw things one way, and I saw them another, is all. I finally stood my ground with her. But you know, we're not mad at each other anymore, honestly. We made up before her mom picked her up."

"Good. I'm glad you two made up. Good friends are important in life. In my book, the mark of a true friendship is when friends can walk in opposite directions, regardless of what the conflict is about, yet remain side by side. I'm proud of you, September. This is something you can write about in your notebook. And don't forget to add that you went to India's soccer tournament, too."

"Okay. I will." There's a pause. "I feel a little sick."

"See there, with all the excitement you had today with Tori's accident, the rain...I should've picked you up when it started to drizzle."

Mom places the palm of her hand on my forehead. "Maybe there's a bug going around. Go lay down, September. You feel warm. No ifs, ands, or buts. To bed."

"All right. I'm going." As I walk toward my room, I look around for Dee-O-Gee; he always comes with me.

"Where's Dee-O-Gee?

"Outside chasing chipmunks!"

Here's what I write in my notebook before I go to sleep Sunday night:

> ## My talents and best qualities
> ## Sunday night
>
> • Went to church. Got sneezed on.
> • Helped mom fold laundry.
> • Went to India's soccer tournament.
> • Held the umbrella over Tori's head to keep rain off her face.
> • Gave Sabeen raincoat for her kitten Ballzac.
> • Covered Tori's piano books so they didn't get wet.
> • Comforted Tori after she got hit in the mouth with the soccer ball until her mom picked her up.
> • Got in argument with Tori but made up.
> • Emailed neighborhood secretary about doggie uh-oh on streets.
> • Told mom I love her before I go to bed.

Chapter 8

Miss Heh-choo

"Good afternoon, September," I hear Mom say. "I just called Mrs. Neuman to check on Tori. She's staying home today, too. She's still bandaged up and pretty sore. She'll be as good as new in a week or so. She says, 'hello.'"

"Okay. Wait. Did you say, 'good afternoon'?"

"Yes."

"What day is it? Heh-choo."

"It's Monday." Mom hands me a box of tissue.

"Why didn't you wake me up for school? Heh-choo." I hold the tissue over my nose.

"You were sick all night. Your temperature was 103.4. Between you and all that thunder and lightning we had last night that I thought would never let up, I didn't get an ounce of sleep. Don't you remember?"

"No. I don't remember the thunder, lightning, or being sick."

"I guess the medicine I gave you made you drowsy," she answers.

"It's Makayla's fault I'm sick. She sneezed on me at church yesterday, remember? Heh-choo." I grab another tissue. Mom shrugs, slips a thermometer in my mouth, and waits a few seconds.

"Let's not forget, you *were* outside in the rain yesterday, too," she says looking straight into my eyes. *Beep beep beep.* She takes the thermometer out of my mouth. "It's down to 100.8; still too high to go to school. You need more rest and some orange juice."

"Oh no! The assignment! Heh-choo." I take another tissue.

"What assignment?"

"You know. The writing assignment. The one that I left on my desk that I didn't start. I covered it because I didn't want anyone to know that I didn't write anything yet. Heh-choo." I sneeze in my arm this time.

"Don't worry about that. I'm sure Mrs. Bridgewaters will take care of everything, the sweetheart that she is. Just get better so you can go back to school."

Mom walks over to her bedroom to answer the phone. She always knows how to cheer me up, but this time nothing she says makes me feel any better. All I can think about is how much everyone is going to make fun of me for not having anything written.

"September, it's your father. I put it on speakerphone in case you have to sneeze you won't do it in his ear," she says, before handing me the phone.

"Hi, Daddy. Heh-choo." I hold the phone away from my face so I don't sneeze on it.

"How's my little angel?" *I like when he calls me that.*

"I'm sick. Heh-choo." I hold it away again.

"So I hear."

"It's Makayla's fault. She sneezed on me at church yesterday... remember?"

"No, I don't remember. I went sightseeing today and bought you a souvenir."

Dad didn't seem to mind that Makayla got me sick so I decide to let it go. Plus all that business about forgiving *and* forgetting from yesterday's sermon...well. "What'd you get me? Heh-choo." I hold the phone away again.

"You'll know in a few days. I'm gonna mail it to you."

"I can't wait to get it! Heh-choo." I hold it away, again!

"Dad."

64

"Yes."

"I have to tell you something." There's a long pause.

"What is it, September?

"Aahhhh."

"Yes. I'm waiting."

"Never mind, I'll tell you later." Why bring up the chipmunk cover-up now and spoil his trip? I'll tell him when he comes home.

"Okay, I hope you feel better soon."

"Thanks, Dad. I love you. Heh-choo." Oops. I sneeze right *on* the phone this time.

"I love you, too, Miss Heh-choo. Goodbye."

Mom's downstairs checking her email messages when I get off the phone. She reads Mrs. Willoughby's message to me. She thanked me for letting her know about the doggie uh-oh in the neighborhood and plans to send a note to everyone reminding them to be responsible.

I take some medicine, drink a glass of orange juice, and head back to bed after she reads the message. "Heh-choo." Thanks, Makayla!

Minutes later, Mom and Dee-O-Gee walk into my room. Mom sits in my rocker and Dee-O-Gee jumps on my bed. I need something to lift my spirits, so I ask Mom to tell me the story of how she and Dad met, as if I hadn't heard it before.

"September, I've told you that story a million times already. I bet you can say it backward."

"Just one more time. Please, Mom. I love listening to it. Please."

"Such a persistent child. You *are* your father's daughter."

We both chuckle.

"Thanks, Mom."

Mom sits back and gets comfortable in the chair. "It was a dark and stormy night, like last night," she laughs.

"Mom."

"Just kidding. It was actually a beautiful autumn day in September," she smiles at the memory.

I interrupt her. "That's why you named me September; it was the month you met your prince charming." We both giggle like little schoolgirls sharing a private joke.

"That's right," she says. "And the month of September is during my favorite time of year, fall. Now where was I? Oh, yes, the air was cool and crisp and the heavenly blue sky made a beautiful backdrop to the colorful foliage on the oak trees that lined the sidewalks. I was enrolled in the University of Pittsburgh's Master's in Teaching Program and your father was a student working on his master's in business administration degree."

"Heh-choo."

Mom stops talking and waits for me to blow my nose. For the moment, there's only my sneezing and silence, with a few Dee-O-Gee snores.

"It was lunchtime and I was waiting in line to buy a hotdog from a street vendor named Brock Lee."

I don't care how many times I've heard his name before; it always makes me laugh.

"While I was standing in line, this handsome young fellow, tall and slender, with light brown eyes and dark wavy hair came and stood directly behind me. He was gorgeous and had a charming smile that was all his own."

"Heh-choo." My sneezing interrupts her again. She waits patiently while I wipe my nose before she goes on. She's a patient mother.

"I ordered my food and realized I was a dollar short. I was embarrassed. This handsome man behind me heard I was a dollar short and offered to give me a dollar. In fact, he insisted. How could I refuse? I was starving and I was holding up the line, not to mention how adamant he was in giving me the dollar. I had no choice but to accept it so I took the dollar, paid Brock, and then thanked him for giving me the money. I insisted that I pay him back. He agreed, so we decided to meet a week later, same time, same spot."

Mom hasn't stopped smiling since she began telling the story.

"A week went by and the day came when I was to meet this handsome fellow again. It had occurred to me that I still didn't know his name. He arrived first and was sitting down on a picnic bench eating lunch. I took one look at him and thought that he was more handsome today than he was a week ago. I approached him with the dollar bill in my hand and said, 'I believe this is yours.' He looked up

66

at me and said, 'What's that for?' I immediately thought to myself, hum, handsome and funny, what a great combination! 'Go on, take it, it's yours', I said. He sat looking at me in the most peculiar way, like he didn't remember me. 'It's the dollar that I owe you from last week, remember?' We must have gone back and forth like this for a while until he finally said, 'Oh, that must have been my brother, Robert, my identical twin.' He looked past me and then said, 'Speak of the devil.' I didn't understand what was going on. I dropped my hand to the side and spun around only to find Robert, your father, standing right behind me. I was speechless.

"A moment later, they both started laughing. I put two and two together and realized I was in a game of let's fool the new girl trick between Robert, your father, and Raymond, your uncle. What they thought was funny at the time I thought was cruel, so I started to walk away. Your father caught up to me and apologized. We didn't officially start dating until six months after that. To this day, your father teases me and says, 'Rosemary Champlin, you owe me a dollar.' Then I say, 'I don't owe you a dollar, I owe Raymond a dollar.' He's right, though. I never did give him the dollar I owed him.

"Over the years I think back to how we met and laugh inside over their plan to trick me. I figured if he went through the trouble to trick me, I must have made an impression on him the first day we met. I learned how to take things in stride, you know, tease him back. It always seems to keep things fun between us."

"Now tell me how he proposed to you."

"September! Really?"

"Yes! I love listening to this story, too. Hold on a second. While you talk I'm gonna jot some things down in my notebook. Heh-choo."

"Bless you."

"Thank you."

"After this I want you to get some rest."

"Okay."

"We were away at a retreat in Sedona, Arizona, and rented a car for the day. Little did I know at the time your father had it all planned. We were out visiting area attractions and drove up a mountain deep with red rock. On our way up the mountain, we actually had to stop to let a herd of cows pass in front of the car. It was hilarious watching these cows with huge bells tied around their necks casually walk in front of us. It wasn't the sort of thing you see every day. Anyway, when we reached the top of the mountain it was dusk and started to drizzle, but the view was spectacular." Mom pauses and turns to look out the window and lowers her voice.

"Your father wanted me to get out of the car and sit on a rock beside him to look out over the city. I didn't want to get out because it started raining harder. He kept begging me to get out, but I kept telling him it was raining too hard. I didn't want to mess up my clothes and especially my *hair*."

She stops and looks directly at me.

"You know what I mean."

I don't, but I smile at her anyway.

"I thought he was going to give up, but I was wrong. That's when I realized how stubborn and persistent he was. By the time he got out of the car it was raining cats and dogs, but he got out anyway, ran to my side, opened the door, and got down on one knee. 'Robert, what's the matter with you?' I asked him. 'It's pouring down rain and you're getting all wet.' He looked a hot mess; his hair was as flat as a pancake. But I didn't tell *him* that. He reached into his pocket and pulled out a box, a black, felt box. My heart started racing. I thought to myself, *He's going to propose,* and he did. He pulled out this ring." She points to her engagement ring. "He held me with his eyes and said, 'Rosemary Lipscomb, will you do me the honor of being my bride?' Tears were flowing down my face when I looked into his gentle eyes and said, 'Yes.' I'll never forget the day we got engaged. We were young, happy, and financially independent with all the world before us."

"Heh, heh, heh, heh-chooooo."

"Bless you."

"Thank you." I blow my nose, then *I* finish telling the story. I've heard it so many times, I can say it blindfolded. "And then you drove down the mountain, but first you had to wait for the same herd of cows that passed in front of you when you drove up the mountain to pass in front of you on your way down the mountain. You went to a restaurant where Daddy already made reservations, and you ate the best she-crab soup you've ever had. Before you left the restaurant, Daddy bought a keepsake, a small wooden ornament of the restaurant to remember the day he proposed to you."

We look at each other before I finish. Mom's still smiling as I say, "and they lived happily ever after. The end."

Here's what I write in my notebook on Monday:

My talents and best qualities
Monday

- I forgave Makayla for coughing on my hands at church.

- I listened to mom's stories about how she met dad and how he proposed to her.

- I let my friends choose the games we play.

- In first grade I once stood up for Sabeen when she was being bullied.

- I let people cut ahead of me in the cafeteria line.

- One Thanksgiving I helped pass out meals at a homeless shelter with my father.

- I listen to what my parents and grandmother tell me to do most of the time.

- I helped Mrs. Bridgewaters bring her gerbils, Winter and Solstice, into her classroom.

Chapter 9

Tuesday Morning

It's Tuesday morning. I've stopped sneezing, but I'm still a little sick. I guess I won't be going to school today. Mom never woke me up, and school has already started.

"Oh please, Lord, no!" Mom screams.

Uh-oh, the chipmunk must have come back into the house! Now I'll be forced to tell the truth. Why isn't Dee-O-Gee barking at it? I run downstairs to help Mom. When I get there, she's not in the kitchen on top of the table; she's in the family room sitting down on the couch in front of the TV. I look at what she's watching. My eyes are about to pop out! I can't believe what I see! People are running, and screaming, and crying through thick, black smoke. It's everywhere! I look at Mom. She's crying with her hands covering her mouth. I dash over to her.

"Mom, what happened?"

She uncovers her mouth and lowers her hands to her lap.

"The pl…p…pla…"

She's crying so hard I can't understand what she's trying to say.

"Mom. Talk slower."

She takes a deep breath and says very slowly, "Two planes cr…

crashed into the wah...World Tra...Trade Towers in...New York City." She adds, "Th...that's close to wh...where your fa...father went...for his b...business meeting." Mom pauses to let her words sink in.

That's when a bomb goes off. KABOOM! I'm hit out of nowhere. My heart nearly stops in my chest. I open my mouth and try to speak. Nothing comes out; I've completely lost my voice. I *must* be dreaming. My head, the room, everything is spinning around me. I feel off balance. I'm falling. I'm falling a million miles away from Earth, watching my life from outside my body.

When the phone rings, I shake my head and come back to myself. That's when I realize this isn't a dream. This is real. Mom answers it and quickly puts it on speakerphone.

"Hello!"

"Sister Rosemary!"

"Pastor!" she cries.

"I just heard the news about the planes crashing into the towers! Robert told me at church that he had a meeting in Lower Manhattan on Tuesday."

Mom's quiet.

"Have you heard from him?"

"Not yet," she says, wiping her tears.

"I'm on my way over with some of the Elders to pray with you."

"Okay." Mom hangs up the phone then turns off the TV. She walks back to the couch, falls to her knees, takes me in her arms and says, "Please God, let him be okay. Please God..." she keeps saying over and over and over.

We still haven't heard from Dad when Pastor Farmer and the Elders show up. Oh, no! Elder Weems came! We'll be here all day praying. We exchange hugs, make a circle, bow our heads, and pray in turn. When we finish, which didn't take as long as I thought 'cause Elder Weems was short-winded today, I ask Mom how the planes crashed into the buildings.

A heavy silence covers the room. Mom seems shaken by my question. She sits me down on the couch and gently clears the frog in her throat.

"September," she pauses a moment like she's deciding something, "let me be very, very clear." She looks around the room and locks eyes with Pastor Farmer. He takes his glasses off, folds his arms, and nods his head in support of what she is going to say. From the serious look on everyone's face, I don't want to listen to her, but I can't keep my ears from hearing. It's like wanting an answer but being afraid to hear it. My heart is in my mouth as she lowers her voice to a whisper and gets right to the point.

"September, sweetheart, they suspect America was attacked by hijackers who caused the planes to crash on purpose."

Her words settle in my mind.

"What's a hijacker?" I question, praying she won't answer me for fear I will learn more than I want to.

"It's someone who tries to take control of a plane, or ship, or car and forces it to go in a different direction."

"But why, Mommy? Why'd they do that?"

"Because some people live to create terror and fear in people's lives," she says, trying to speak calmly.

"But why'd God allow them to do something that horrible?"

"I don't know, sweetheart. I really—don't—know. I don't have a good explanation. Just that sometimes God allows things to happen that don't make sense to us."

"I don't understand. Why'd He allow something so terrible like this to happen?" I cry.

I look at her and wait for her to say something, anything.

"His thoughts aren't our thoughts, and His ways aren't our ways. All we can do is trust in Him, September."

She opens her arms and pulls me close to her. I'm sad, confused, and all my questions haven't been answered. Mainly because I'm too afraid to ask them. But while streams of tears roll down my face, I somehow feel at peace knowing that God will take care of Dad… wherever he is.

It's late afternoon. Half the city of Pittsburgh is sitting in our living room. You'd think Dad was some sort of a hero, a celebrity, or something from all the soft laughter mixed with whispers and quiet conversations I hear about him. I've got so much time on my hands;

I float around the room and catch bits and pieces of what people are saying.

"He mowed my mother's grass," "helped in the soup kitchen," "painted our fence," "drove the van," "shoveled our driveway," "helpful," "kind," "dependable," "honest," "understanding."

Story after story, memory after memory, reflection after reflection. The more I listen, the more I feel like they're talking as if my father's dead. That's the only time people say nice things about someone: when they're dead.

Wait—a—minute! My father's not dead. He just hasn't called yet, but he will. He promised he'd take me somewhere special when he gets back. Robert Champlin always keeps his promises. That's what I'd scream at them if I felt like it. Or if I was brave enough. I wish everyone would just go home.

Hours have gone by and still no call from Dad. Lots of women from our church have shown up with food. Who can eat at a time like this? It smells so good, though. It reminds me of the holidays, like Thanksgiving or Christmas. Mom tells me to get something to eat since I haven't eaten all day. I walk into the kitchen. My stomach starts growling as my eyes roam around at the spread of food on the table. There's enough food here to feed an army.

Mrs. McCall was my first Sunday school teacher and she's also the best cook at our church. She's a better cook than Mom, but I've never told her that. Her Kool-Aid's way too sweet, though. But the way she makes her baked chicken, macaroni and cheese, and collard greens is from another world. She hands me a plate of food.

"Thank you, Mrs. McCall."

"You're welcome, Sugar."

I'm tired after dinner. Sitting around doing nothing takes a lot of energy out of me. I say goodnight to everyone, give Mom a really long hug, then head to my room. Dee-O-Gee follows me. I drag my hand very slowly on the banister as I walk upstairs and look at our family pictures on the wall. I've walked by them a thousand times but never really noticed them. When I'm sad and bored, I pay attention to things.

On my way down the upstairs hall, I walk into my parents' room and open my mom's dresser drawer lined with sheets of lavender-scented paper. I push my hands through her clothes and rub them on the paper at the bottom of the drawer. I stick my head down in the drawer and inhale slowly…very slowly. I exhale even more slowly. I'm hoping the aroma of the lavender will take my pain away since it's supposed to relax you. When I've had enough, I close the drawer then head to my room. I leave the door cracked in case Dee-O-Gee wants to go downstairs during the night. I don't bother brushing my teeth, getting undressed, or even writing in my notebook. I crawl in bed and pull the covers clear up to my chin. Dee-O-Gee takes his place in his usual spot next to my feet.

I hear the front door open and shut way past midnight. I wait for the sound of the door to open again, but it never comes. Everyone must be gone. I found it comforting listening to the softness of their voices downstairs.

Now that they're gone, I'm left with my thoughts. I try to think of reasons why Dad hasn't called yet. *Maybe he lost his phone. But if he lost it, why doesn't he borrow someone else's? Maybe he's trapped somewhere yelling for help and no one can hear him. Or maybe he's…* I stop myself from saying what I'm thinking. It's too much for me to handle. I raise my hands to my face and breathe in the fading fragrance.

I'm still restless and can't fall asleep. Dee-O-Gee fell asleep hours ago. I try burying my face under my covers, but I immediately feel like I'm suffocating and quickly pull the covers from my head.

I've dozed on and off throughout the night, but now I'm wide awake and notice a soft glow of light coming from my parents' room. *Is Dad home?* Visions of him fill my mind. *Was he tired when he got home and didn't have the energy to turn the light off? Did he and Mom drift off to sleep while talking with the light on?*

I jump off my bed and disturb Dee-O-Gee's sleep. He jumps off, too, and runs downstairs. I dash toward the light across the hall and burst into the room to find Mom sleeping in her chair with a picture of our family resting between her hands. There's no sign Dad has returned; I don't see his luggage. I check their closet and bathroom just to be sure. I even look under their bed, knowing full well Dad's not there. I needed to be sure.

Should I wake her and help her to bed, or should I leave her be? I'll leave her be. No use in both of us worrying. I walk toward Mom, pull the picture from her hands, and stare at it a moment. We took this picture this summer on our vacation at Kiawah Island. I can still hear the sound of the ocean waves crashing up against the sandy beach. I place the picture on top of Mom's dresser and then open the drawer to get more lavender on my hands. I quietly turn her light off, walk to my room, and slip back in bed. I close my eyes and see my father smiling at me. I drift to sleep.

Chapter 10

A Change in Me

An anxious feeling mixed with the smell of coffee wakes me the next day. I'm too afraid to go downstairs. I don't want to hear bad news about Dad, if there is any. I put some music on low and stay in bed for a while thinking about Dad and the things we've done together.

Like the time he took me to my first Pirates baseball game. I ate a hotdog, cotton candy, *and* peanuts in the shells. There were fireworks after the game. They were so beautiful the way they lit up the sky. I don't even remember if the Pirates won or lost—I didn't care, I was with my dad.

Then there was the time he gave me five dollars when I lost my first tooth. He barely gave me enough time to fall asleep. I had to pretend I was sleeping with fake snores when he sneaked into my room and put the money under my pillow.

And I'll never forget the time we went to Kennywood Amusement Park and rode on the Thunderbolt rollercoaster fives times. For a snack, we shared an order of fries from the Potato Patch. Man, were they good!

Thinking about the good times gives me the courage to finally go downstairs. I turn the music off and head downstairs. I approach the kitchen and hear the mellow sound of people talking. I recognize Mom's voice, but who's she talking to? It's a male voice, but who is it? I can't make it out. Is it Dad? My heart beats faster and faster the closer I get to them. I squint trying to look around the corner into the kitchen. I freeze at the entrance.

"Daddy!" I think I startled him. He turns and looks at me. "You did come home!"

I run over to him and jump into his arms. I want to ask him a thousand questions, but first I'm gonna give him a piece of my mind for not calling us, after I tell him how much I love him. Wait. Something's wrong.

"No, September," Mom answers quickly, taking her eyes off her coffee cup. "It's not your father, it's Uncle Raymond."

The doorbell rings; Dee-O-Gee starts barking and sprints to the front door. Mom follows him.

I lean back in his arms and take a second to study his face. Yep, it's Uncle Raymond's face all right. He has more freckles and a hairier face than Dad. As I stare at him, all the energy I have in my body leaves, kind of like watching a balloon deflate. I try not to act too disappointed that Uncle Raymond isn't Dad, but I'm not successful.

"Oh, it is you."

"It's okay, September," he whispers, "I understand. You can give old Uncle Raymond a hug anyway."

"I thought you were Dad. You look just like him," I whisper back, as the story of how my parents met flashes in my mind.

I allow my thoughts to wander and find myself thinking: *Maybe Dad and Uncle Raymond are up to their old tricks again. Maybe Uncle Raymond isn't Uncle Raymond but is really Dad pretending to be Uncle Raymond. Would they do something that mean?* I immediately let go of this thought because that wouldn't be a trick at all, that would be cruel, and Dad's not like that—stubborn maybe, but not cruel.

"When did you get here?" I ask, as we stop hugging each other.

"After midnight."

"Did Aunt Sylvia, Jayden, and Cameron come with you?"

"Just me," he says, pouring himself a cup of coffee. He pours in a lot more cream than coffee, just like Dad. Mom and Pastor Farmer walk into the kitchen; his face is unshaven.

"Hello, Pastor," Uncle Raymond says, shaking Pastor Farmer's hand. "Been a while."

"It has. How's your family?"

"Everyone's fine."

"Good, good."

"And yours?"

"Doing well. Thanks for asking." Pastor Farmer turns to me.

"And how are you, September?" he says, placing a firm hand on my shoulder.

"I'm okay," I say, lying through my teeth. I feel horrible. I'm surprised I can keep a straight face.

"Care for some coffee, Pastor?" Mom asks. "Oh, I almost forgot, you prefer hot water to tea and coffee. Let me get you a cup."

"Thank you," he replies.

Mom pours Pastor Farmer a cup of hot water. "Would you like a slice of lemon?" He's the only person I know who drinks hot water.

"Plain water is fine. Thanks."

Mom hands him the mug.

"Thank you."

"You're welcome."

Pastor Farmer cups his hands around the mug and blows into it. It's very hot.

"A fine cup of water. That's very hospitable of you, Sister Rosemary."

"Thank you, Pastor."

"Hospitable? What's that mean?" I ask.

"It means your mother is a good host, September. She's generous. And she's using her generosity for the benefit of others. That's a gift from the Almighty. A person who's hospitable means that they're cordial or they know how to take care of guests in their home."

"Oh. Is it like having a talent or special ability?" I ask.

"On a general level, yes, it is. You see, people are born with certain talents, natural abilities, or… or… or…skills, like singing, playing an instrument, painting, running, throwing, playing basketball, listening to a friend's problem, deciding what clothes to wear, pretty much any ability that comes easily or naturally to them. We typically engage in activities that support our talents."

"Okay, sooo, *I* was born with *talents*?"

"Why of course you were, September. You're a sweet young lady. I notice how you always hold the door for people when they come to church. That means you're considerate of others. We need to get you on the Greeters' Committee." We all laugh.

"And that's a talent?"

"Why, certainly! A person can have all kinds of talents. Talents aren't limited to special abilities in sports, music, or art. A talented person is responsible, a problem solver, persuasive, an achiever, has empathy. I can go on and on, September. Are you grasping any of this?"

"I think I am. Yes. I think I am. Thanks, Pastor Farmer."

"You're welcome, September."

"No need to stand up and talk! Why don't we all have a seat?" Mom asks.

She wipes the crumbs off the table from last night's feast before we sit down. Pastor Farmer raises his mug to his mouth before deciding it's still too hot. He puts his mug down, then takes his glasses off his face and places them next to his mug. The water's so hot it completely fogs his glasses; then they get all wet. Uncle Raymond is less concerned about drinking his coffee. He smoothes out the wrinkles in the tablecloth then pulls at his whiskers.

I glance at Mom. Doesn't look like she got any sleep last night with her orange and yellow flowered scarf tied crooked around her head and those brown bags under her eyes and all. I probably *should have* helped her into bed last night. I don't care what she looks like; she's the most beautiful woman in the world to me. While I stare at her, I overhear Pastor Farmer say something to Uncle Raymond about an adoption. When I get up from my chair to give Mom a hug, I notice a large white envelope on the kitchen counter addressed to me.

"Where'd that envelope come from?"

"Mrs. Bridgewaters brought it by last night. You were sleeping and I didn't want to wake you. I called her yesterday and told her about your father."

"What's in it?"

"I don't know. I didn't open it. It's addressed to you."

I look at it suspiciously, reach down, and slowly pick it up. I open it and pull out some papers. Homework? I can't believe it. My father is missing and Mrs. Bridgewaters brings me homework to do! *Would she stoop that low?* When I look closer, I notice lots of writing on the page. I start reading the paper. Turns out all my classmates wrote something special to me.

They say things like:

You're the most helpful person I know. Thanks for helping me pick up the books. That meant a lot to me. ~Isaiah

You're caring and gentle with animals—especially kittens whose middle names are Mr. Gigglesworth. You're a great friend! ~Sabeen

You're friendly and fun to be with. ~Tori

Hang in there. ~Houston

You're a team player. Thanks for watching my soccer game in the rain. ~India

Thanks for not laughing at me. ~Mercedes

Even Mrs. Bridgewaters wrote something. She said, *I've watched you blossom over the years at Three Rivers. You're a leader with a big heart. ~Mrs. Bridgewaters.*

I start to feel differently about myself when I read what they wrote to me. It's kinda funny how people like Pastor Farmer, Mrs. Bridgewaters, and even my classmates help me realize there are lots of ways to be talented. I might not be athletic, play an instrument, or even be smart. But I am friendly, respectful, and helpful, and those are important qualities, too! Their words make a change in me. I begin to feel good about myself and believe that nothing will ever make me feel like an airhead or average again. The *best* thing is that the words "airhead" and "average" slowly fade from my mind. For the first time in my life I feel strong, confident, and brave. The way Ruby Bridges looked when she walked through the screaming crowds of people in the book Judge Bridgewaters read to us.

The phone rings. Mom answers it and immediately puts it on speakerphone.

"Rosemary Champlin?"

"This is she."

"Mrs. Champlin, my name is Dr. Okafor. I'm an emergency room doctor from New York Downtown Hospital in New York City." The four of us hold our breath as we stare at the phone.

"I have news about your husband, ma'am. Mrs. Champlin, your husband, Robert Champlin, was found dead in one of the World Trade Towers. He died of smoke inhalation while helping the police and fire fighters rescue people trapped in the north tower at the World Trade Center Tuesday morning, September 11th. Your husband kept going back into the flames, pulling people out, saving their lives. He risked his own life to save the lives of seven…eight people. From what I was told, he was very assiduous. He was determined to go back in, time and time again."

Mom's voice cracks and is almost in a whisper when she asks the doctor if Dad had his inhaler in his pocket.

"The only things found on him, ma'am, were his wallet and his keys. If I may add, ma'am, your husband, Robert Champlin, died a hero."

Mom drops the phone and collapses on the floor. I want to catch her, but I can't. My feet are frozen to the floor. Dee-O-Gee's startled and runs outta the kitchen. Uncle Raymond spills his coffee on the table rushing to catch Mom. Pastor Farmer watches in horror. A heavy weight falls on my ears and stays there. My ears are ringing and are hot—not to the touch, but on the inside. I have to go somewhere I feel safe. My legs are wiggly like spaghetti noodles, but I run lightning-fast to my room and lock my door. I don't want anyone to come in, no one! I throw myself on my bed and cry for a very, very, very long time.

When I wake up, Mom and Dee-O-Gee are in my room. Dee-O-Gee's licking my feet, and Mom's in my rocking chair with a blanket covering her.

"Hello, sweetheart," she says softly, rocking back and forth…

back and forth…back and forth.

"Hi," I whisper.

I wiggle my legs to stop Dee-O-Gee from licking my feet. Now they're all wet. He stops, yawns, and then starts licking his own paws. When he finishes, he rests his head back on my legs. Silly dog. He thinks he's one of us. Well, actually…

"How'd you get in here?"

"With this." She holds up a bobby pin.

"Oh."

We don't say a word after that. Mom sticks the bobby pin underneath her scarf, folds the blanket down onto her lap, and then stares out the window looking at the cloudless sky, watching some birds in a nearby tree. She seems lost within herself. I'll bet she doesn't even hear the birds calling each other. It's like she doesn't really see or hear anything.

I turn to look at my ceiling and stare at a small brown splotch that must've come from the heavy rain we had the other day. I stare at it for a while before I start thinking about my friends. I wonder what they'd do if they were me right now. Sabeen would read a book to make her feel better. Correction, she'd read three or four books to make her feel better. India would kick a soccer ball around in her backyard or play basketball in her driveway. And Tori would play the piano, or violin, take a math test, or somethin'. Me? I don't do anything but stare at a brown splotch.

"I'm sad…and angry."

"Go on," Mom says. As always, her words are tenderly spoken.

"I'm sad because Dad's gone. And I'm angry because he died helping the fire fighters do *their* job. If he hadn't helped them, he'd still be alive."

"You're probably right. That's the kind of person he was…always helping other people," she says with *no* anger in her voice.

"Mom."

"Yes."

I hesitate.

"I'm listening."

"Do you believe in silly prayers?"

"What do you mean?"

"I told God I'm angry at him. It feels sort of silly to pray that way."

"Did it help you feel better?"

"Kind of," I say, staring at the splotch.

"Then it's okay."

It's silent again. I'm thinking over her words, the reassurance in her voice.

"Mom."

"Ah-ha."

"Is Dad in heaven?"

She stops rocking, leans up in the chair, and looks me straight in the eyes. Her big brown eyes are filled with heavy tears. "What does your heart tell you?" she asks in a lavender-like voice.

My heart? My heart's been in my mouth for the last two days. I'd forgotten I had one. I rest my hand over it to make sure it's still there before I answer,

"That he's in heaven."

"Then that, my dear, is where he is."

She leans back in the chair and continues to rock back and forth... back and forth.

"Follow your heart, September, just follow your heart," she squeaks out under her breath as buckets full of tears roll down her face.

Do her eyes burn from crying, too? I ask myself.

"Would you like to talk about anything else?" she asks, wiping her face with wet hands.

"No."

"I'm here when you want to."

I nod. "Where are Uncle Raymond and Pastor Farmer?"

"Pastor Farmer left hours ago. Said he had a meeting with an adoption agency. Uncle Raymond's downstairs making phone calls. By the way, a little bird told me your grandmother's on her way from Detroit and will be here by nightfall. She'll stay with us. Everyone else from both sides of the family, Aunt Lucinda, Uncle Eric, Aunt Diane, and all the rest of your aunts, uncles, and cousins are staying in a hotel. They'll be here within the next few days. Come on. Let's get the guest room ready for Grandma."

"I'll be down in a minute."

"Okay."

A little bird told her? Maybe I was wrong about Mom after all and she really *did* hear the birds calling each other in the trees. Mom cradles me in her arms for a while, then heads for the door and disappears in the hallway. I give brother dog a hug, too, before he springs off the bed and follows her. He stops when he gets to the door and looks back at me.

"Don't worry boy, I'll be okay."

He shakes his tail, turns, and catches up with Mom. Dee-O-Gee's no dummy. He knows who makes for better company right now.

I sit on my bed with my legs dangled over the side watching the sun smile. Its bright, thin rays spread evenly across my bedroom floor. Clear, feathery dust floats through the air and settles around the room. I want to go downstairs, but my mind won't let me. It's stuck on a thought: *how awful it is to be the exact age and named after the month that took my father's life.* If I wasn't eleven and if I had a regular name like Brittany, Taylor, Megan, or Kiara, I wouldn't feel this way. The month of September marks the beginning of so many things: a new season of color, the fall, Mom's favorite time of year, a new school year, *and* the Jewish New Year, Rosh Hashanah. Tori celebrates this holiday with her family by eating apples dipped in honey; it represents the start of a sweet new year.

Now the month of September represents the end of life—for me and lots of other people, too. I miss my father so much, I'm angry. Just angry! I grab the closest thing to me, my writing assignment, and rip it to shreds. The assignment that I put so much time and effort into is now a pile of trash on my bedroom floor. I don't even care! Only here's what I don't get. *Why do I feel good being angry?*

I'm so confused right now. I'm not even sure if the sound of some distant church bells is real or in my mind. I barely have the energy to drag myself off my bed, walk over to my window, and listen carefully to the birds call each other.

"Tweet? That you? Can you hear me?"

I wait for a response. I wonder—as I listen to the sweet melodies—if I'll ever sing like that again.

Chapter 11

A Wish Come True

After Dad's funeral, a candlelight vigil is held at Bethany Baptist in honor of him and other people who risked their lives during the September 11th attacks on America. Hundreds of people are here but I hardly recognize anyone. The only people I know are family members, teachers, neighbors, and friends, like Mrs. Jenkins and Nathaniel. I look past a gathering crowd of people and see Tori, Sabeen, and India standing together. They help me pass out candles to everyone as they arrive.

Pastor Farmer opens the ceremony with a word of prayer. Then Reverend Fuller of First AME Church talks briefly about September 11th. I snuggle close to Grandma while he talks. Mom's on the other side wiping her eyes and dabbing her nose with a wet, soggy tissue. Uncle Raymond, Aunt Sylvia, Jayden, and Cameron sit next to Mom. I purposely turn my body away from Uncle Raymond; I'm creeped out looking at him since he looks just like Dad.

I don't pay attention to everything during the ceremony, but I do remember one thing Reverend Fuller says: "The purpose of this gathering is not to mourn death, but to celebrate life. Focus on remembering all the good times you shared with your loved ones and don't dwell on how they lost their lives."

After his speech, we light the candles. It's spooky as they light up in the dark. Hundreds of lights flicker brightly in the cool evening air. Pastor Farmer asks for a moment of silence…then we sing "This Little Light of Mine." It was one of Dad's favorite songs.

We blow our candles out at the end of the song, then a swarm of people gather around my family and tell us how sorry they are for our loss. This makes Mom cry harder. Not me. I refuse to. If I start crying, I won't stop. For some reason everyone's presence here tonight has somehow softened the hurt of my father's death. And in a way, I feel reassured in knowing that all these people care for Mom and me, even if they don't really know us.

Mom put me in charge of collecting all the cards everyone brought us. When we get home, we open them and find that lots of people who don't even know us have given us money. I'm blown away. Most cards don't have a return address. Cards sent in the mail come from as far as Florida, Maryland, Connecticut, and Michigan, and as near as Butler and New Kensington, Pennsylvania.

Grandma stays with us a few days longer. Good thing. Some days Mom doesn't even get out of bed. Grandma's done all the house cleaning and some cooking. Her cooking's not bad, but not as good as Mrs. McCall's either. Glad there are still some leftovers. I help wash clothes. It's what Dad would have wanted me to do.

When the president of the United States hears about what my Dad did, he invites us to the White House. I can't believe we're going to meet President Bush, just like Mrs. Bridgewaters. It's like a wish come true.

There are lots of other families invited to come, too. We're given a tour of the White House and then escorted to the East Room for the program. The East Room is very fancy. The walls are fancy, the floor is fancy, the mirrors are fancy, the piano is fancy, the windows are fancy, and three enormous chandeliers hang from a very fancy ceiling. There's even a huge picture of George Washington on a wall and a picture of his wife, Martha, in a fancy dress.

We find two seats in the first row of chairs. I'm extremely nervous and roll the program I'm holding in my hand into a telescope and peer through it—looking at the picture of George Washington on the wall.

"September, mind your manners," Mom says in a loving voice.

The gentle way she says my name causes me to lower it. Then my foot starts tapping against the floor. Mom reaches over and rests her hand on my leg. That helps, until my other foot starts tapping. I scrunch my toes in my shoes to try to keep them from tapping, and then I start biting my fingernails. Goodness. I'm running out of things to do while we wait for...okay, here we go. President Bush is announced into the room.

When he comes in, he stands on a small stage and welcomes us to his home. He looks shorter in person than he does on TV—with a *whole* lot more gray hair. He declares, "There's been a change in September." He pauses.

I perk up, and suddenly I'm less nervous. Mom glances at me and gives a half smile. I can tell we're thinking the same thing; the president said my name! He's a little choked up, but keeps on talking.

"The men and women whom we honor here today are heroes and are most deserving of this medal of valor for the bravery they displayed on September 11, 2001. There is no higher expression of love than someone who sacrifices his or her own life to help a stranger or country. It demonstrates the utmost extent of loyalty and allegiance."

Although the president is way too short for the NBA, listening to him talk, he stands like a giant at least ten feet tall. He goes on to say lots of other nice things about our loved ones. The more he talks, the more it reminds me of the special things my friends said in the messages they wrote to me.

His words are encouraging. They're so uplifting they make me feel strong, and just like that, my dreams of being president come back to me and all those things I thought were crazy about why I couldn't be president become unimportant. I think to myself... *maybe I won't be president, but that doesn't mean I can't dream I will be someday.*

After the president finishes his speech, he greets his guests, one family at a time. I've got butterflies in my stomach. When it's our turn to meet him, I can almost taste the butterflies in my mouth. Mom shakes his hand when she introduces us. I shake his hand, too, then show him a picture of my family taken at Kiawah Island this summer. He gives me a hug and tells me that my father was a brave and courageous man. I thank him and think back to the story of Ruby Bridges and how brave she was, too.

"That's some teacher you have," President Bush says. My mind tells me he's talking about Mrs. Bridgewaters, but my lips blurt out the only word that comes to my mind. "Who?"

"Mrs. Bridgewaters. I remember her from last year when she received the Teacher of the Year Award."

My mouth turns to jello. "Oh. Yes ma'am...I, I, I, mean sir...I mean, Mr. President. She's my favorite teacher." He realizes how nervous I am and isn't even offended by my mistake.

"She spoke very highly of your father in the letter."

I'm afraid of what'll pop out of my mouth, so I tell myself to *think before you speak.* My voice cracks, but I manage to pull myself together. "No offense, Mr. President, but what letter?"

"The letter about your father. She talked about his fine qualities as a person as well as the sacrifice he made. That's why I invited you and your mother to come to the White House. She also mentioned that you were a lot like him." The president's response takes us by surprise.

"Oh. She did." There's an awkward pause. Mom and I look at each other. Her jaw drops as she mouths the words, "Mrs. Bridgewaters wrote a letter to the president." She drops her jaw again. We had no idea Mrs. Bridgewaters wrote a letter to the president about Dad. She's always doing nice things for other people.

After we get over the shock of what Mrs. Bridgewaters did, I become less nervous and feel comfortable talking with the president.

At the conclusion of the program, we're handed a red, white, or blue balloon and asked to write a message on a note card attached to the balloon.

Mom writes:

> *My Dearest Robert, I will truly miss you. Your strength will help me carry on. Until we meet again. Love, Rosemary*

"I don't want to share what I wrote with you, Mom. Is that okay?"

"That's fine, September. You don't have to share. I respect your privacy."

When we've completed our messages, we're escorted to the White House lawn to release the balloons. Each one of us stands silently as we watch the balloons fade higher and higher in the sky until they're going...going...going...gone. After that we take pictures with the president. Our plan is to put them on the wall with our family photos when we get home.

On our train ride back to Pittsburgh, I finally decide to tell Mom the gospel-honest truth about the chipmunk cover-up. I can't keep it to myself any longer. The worst part is that I never found the courage to tell Dad the truth about what really happened.

"Mom. I have to tell you something about the chipmunk that was in the house."

"What is it, September?"

"Well...I sorta never took it to Frick Park to let it go."

"You didn't? What'd you do?"

"Well...after I poured myself a glass of orange juice, I walked back to the trap and found that it was gone. I only pretended that it was still in the cage just so Dad and I could go to the Vintage Center with Nathaniel. I've felt horrible ever since, just awful not telling anyone about it."

"Life is full of surprises, isn't it, September? I have a little confession of my own."

"What?"

"After you and your father left, I came back downstairs because

Dee-O-Gee was barking up a storm. When I walked into the kitchen, there it was, cornered. It wasn't going anywhere. I had to take matters into my own hands, so I did the only thing I knew, given the circumstances."

"What'd you do?"

"I was terrified, but I had to keep my wits about me so I put my oven mittens on, grabbed my shirt, you know the one that I just bought. It was the first thing I saw in arm's length. I crept up to the chipmunk and flung my shirt over it. Oddest thing. It didn't move. It was like it wanted to be caught. Anyway, I twisted the shirt around him and tied a knot, good and tight. You should have heard Dee-O-Gee barking. Girl, he was out—of—control. I ran to the garage, put it in a box, and closed the lid. Then I threw your father's toolbox in the car. After that I got in my car, drove to Frick Park, and let it go."

"How'd you let it go?"

"You haven't seen my new shirt around the house have you?"

"No."

"I cut it."

"The chipmunk?"

"No. My shirt. I cut my shirt and he scurried away."

"So you've known all along. You knew I never let the chipmunk out of the trap."

"I've known all along, September."

"Did Dad know, too?"

"Yes, I told him."

"Why didn't you tell me that you knew?"

"We wanted *you* to tell us. It was *your* responsibility. Not ours."

"I'm sorry, Mom. I'm really sorry…about everything."

"I know you are, September. What's done is done. That's in the past. We've been through a lot these last few weeks. It's time we turn our eyes to the future."

Chapter 12

Two Blossoming Readers

After we get back from the White House, Mom enrolls me in a support group called Hanna Ann's House—a place where kids can talk about their feelings with other kids when their mom or dad dies or gets really sick. I made a new friend here. Her name's Destiny. Her mom's really sick.

I like going because my counselor, Mrs. Redmen, doesn't *force* me to talk about my feelings if I don't want to. I can sit and listen to other kids talk all day if I want. She says if I talk that's fine, and if I don't talk that's fine, too. She also says it's okay for us to keep our loved ones alive in our hearts and in our minds.

That sounds like something an adult would say. Only problem is—I don't want my father in my mind or in my heart; I want him *here* with me.

"September's going back to school next week, everyone," Mrs. Redmen says to the group.

A few kids clap their hands. Destiny smiles.

"Remember, September, if you find yourself at the end of your rope, don't let go. Tie a knot, sweetheart, and hold on." I continue nodding.

It's early October when I return to school. Lots of my friends give me a hug when they see me. Well, at least the girls do. The boys just say, "Hi, September," or "Welcome back"—that is, everyone except Real-to-Real.

"Hey, September," he says, strolling over to me with his hands in his pockets.

"Hi Real…I mean, Houston."

He's quiet for a second, and then he tilts his head to the side, looking at me with those dimples. "Where do ants go on vacation?" he asks with a grin on his face.

I frown and say, "I don't know. Where do they go?"

"F-r-a-n-t-s. Get it? They go to Frants," he says, and then strolls away with his hands still stuck in his pockets.

I shake my head and watch him take his seat, but not before he tells a knock-knock joke to DeShawn. DeShawn cracks up and then grabs Real-to-Real and gives him a noogie. Those two clowns will never change.

I slowly turn and look down at my desk. I'm surprised to find the papers on top of my desk the same way I left them the first week of school. Nobody touched them. Not even Real-to-Real. What a relief!

I'm quiet for most of the day. I don't feel like talking with anyone, not Mr. George, the school counselor, or even my best friends, who I avoid looking at. I won't be able to ignore them too much longer though; they know me. But until that time comes, I've found comfort in rubbing my fingers over the words *Daddy's Little Angel* on the charm bracelet Dad sent me from New York City. The reverse side reads *Made in USA*.

At the end of the day, I find the strength to tell Mrs. Bridgewaters what happened to my writing assignment.

"Mrs. Bridgewaters?"

"Yes, September."

"I did everything you wanted me to. Please believe me. I wrote on Friday, Saturday, and Sunday night. I even wrote on Monday. But when I heard the news about my dad," I stop and take a deep breath,

"I got so angry that I ripped my writing assignment to shreds." Mrs. Bridgewaters looks at me with forgiving eyes. She reaches for my hand.

"I understand, September. Let's put the assignment on hold…"

"I'd rather not. I'd like to finish it."

"You sure?"

"Yes, I'm sure."

"Then let's do this. I'm certain the assignment helped jog your memory about things you've done for others in the past and in the present, right?"

"Yes."

"Then you have everything you need to describe what your talents or best qualities are, September. It's all right here." She points to my head. "And here." She points toward my heart. She lets go of my hand but I still want to talk with her.

"Mrs. Bridge…"

RING. School's over! Time to go home.

"Good afternoon, boys and girls," Mr. Lang announces. "Please listen carefully to today's announcements. Due to low sales, we've decided to extend the wrapping paper and cookie dough fundraiser sale. A flyer pertaining to the extension will be sent home in Friday folders. Get back out there and sell, sell, sell! First grade, all permission slips for Dawson's Pumpkin Patch are due this Friday. Fifth grade is going to Clarion for the Autumn Leaf Festival on Thursday. Don't forget to pack a lunch; you'll be eating at Cook Forest. Please be on time. The buses will leave promptly at 6:00 a.m. Finally, all kindergarten students will have a vision test tomorrow. Remember the thought for the week: *blossom into an independent reader, writer, and thinker.* That concludes the announcements for today. All safety patrols are on post."

"Goodbye, children, have a good day," Mrs. Bridgewaters says, then, as expected, points to her READ pin.

I pause and stare at her with my mouth slightly open. I don't know what it is, it's hard for me to explain, but as irritating as that gesture is to me, I know in my heart Mrs. Bridgewaters wants what's best for me.

So I've made a decision. I'm going to follow my heart. Somehow I'll find a way to let go of this…this rebellion—that's not the right word—this hatred I have toward reading, and give in to…somehow *learn* how to accept the things in life that I can't change.

I deliberately gather my belongings slowly and wait for everyone to leave before I say goodbye to Mrs. Bridgewaters. When we're alone, she walks over to me. I've been fighting back my tears all day and can't hold back any longer. Neither can she. She takes me into her arms and tells me everything's going to be all right. I feel awkward crying with my teacher. I've never seen a teacher cry before. I didn't even know they did that, especially Mrs. Bridgewaters. She's always smiling. We stop hugging, I wipe my nose with the back of my hand, and then she tells me a story.

"Do you remember the story I told you when I invited my whole class to my party and no one came except for my teacher, Mrs. Harris?"

I nod.

"Well, I never told you, or your class, the present she gave me." Mrs. Bridgewaters pauses and looks down at her pin. "She gave me this." She points to her *READ* pin. "This pin has been a source of inspiration to me, and others, ever since I received it over fifty years ago. It's inspired me, my children, my children's children, and my students for many, many years." She lifts my chin. "I wear it to inspire *all* my students, including you, September," she says softly. "When Mrs. Harris gave it to me, she told me that if I do what it says, it'd be like giving myself a gift over and over again."

There goes that word again, *gift*.

Mrs. Bridgewaters pauses. "It's kind of like rewarding yourself."

Then she told me all the gifts I'll receive.

"The gift of happiness, the gift of satisfaction, *and,* most important, the gift of knowledge. All these types of gifts are far more valuable than any material gift you'll ever receive because they're more meaningful and will stay with you throughout your life. The gift of knowledge is especially important because when you have knowledge, you have power. And when you have power, it makes you a strong person and you're able to deal with anything life throws your way." She lowers her voice. "Including going to school the follow-ing day to face all those kids who didn't come to my birthday party. I just look at it this way: if you don't read, you won't have power, but if you do read, you will have power. If there's one thing I've learned from all my years as a teacher, it's this: literature is a power-ful medium because it offers us personal stories and insight about ourselves." She pauses, then says in her teacher voice, "In order to receive a gift, you must accept it first, right?"

I nod.

"How do you feel when you receive a gift?"

"Happy…good," I say, wiping tears from my eyes.

"That's exactly how I feel. Now, what types of books do you like to read the most? Think about that for a moment while I tell you the types of books I like to read."

Mrs. Bridgewaters's question has piqued my curiosity 'n stuff like that. I've never been asked that before. That's not true; I have been asked that question before, but I never felt that the teachers were interested, *really* interested, in hearing what I had to say. They seemed more concerned with gathering the information than do-ing anything with it. 'Here, September, read this. Here, September, read that,' they'd say, pushing books on me that *they* thought I'd like to read, rather than books that *I* wanted to read. Mrs. Bridgewa-ters is different; she seems like she *genuinely* wants to help me find books that I'm interested in reading to help me become a reader.

"I like reading stories that have believable plots," she says. "And I especially like stories that speak to me about myself and my life, books that resonate with me as an African American woman. Don't get me wrong, I like other types of books, too, from non-fiction to science fiction and mysteries. But when I read realistic stories, I feel they give me hope and strength to face all the problems life throws my way. They make me feel good inside. Now, what kind of teacher would I be if I didn't want that same experience for my students?" She pauses and lowers her voice. "All of my students, September. Okay, kiddo, I'm ready to hear the answer to my ques-tion. What types of books do you like to read the most?"

Mrs. Bridgewaters looks at me very closely. Her eyes are

sparkling.

I clear my throat and say confidently, "I like realistic fiction the most, but I also like historical fiction and fantasies. I prefer stories that have characters who look, act, and sound like me. I'm interested in stories about music, growing up, stories about courage, friendships, and family relationships. Oh, and I'd also like to read short biographies about famous people."

"Very good, now we're getting somewhere. Have you ever read any books like these that you *absolutely* enjoyed?"

"No."

"I know they're out there. We have library tomorrow. The two of us will spend time looking for these types of books. Okay?"

"Okay."

"Good deal. The only way you'll be able to experience true happiness is when you start reading books that *you* find interesting. And the only way you'll find that out is simply by picking up a book and reading it. I want you to become an independent reader, September. I know you can do it. I'm here to help you every step of the way."

I nod. Moments later, we hear talking coming from the hallway. We walk into the hall to find India, Sabeen, and Tori waiting to walk home with me. They overheard everything. I give them all a hug and thank them for waiting. Tori reaches into her backpack, smiles, and hands me a smashed-up bouquet of dried lavender flowers. I reach to take it and notice her face looks a lot better. She's not wearing any bandages, but she has lots of scars. Her wobbly tooth finally came out. Now there're two holes on either side of her mouth. I'm guessing when all her baby teeth fall out she'll get a fake tooth put in.

"We pitched in and bought this for you," she says.

"It was Tori's idea," says India.

"We know how much you like the smell," Sabeen chimes in.

"Aahh. Thank you." I smell it and, you know, it does take some of my pain away. Or maybe it's just being with my best friends and my favorite teacher that makes me feel a little better. It's also kind of nice to see Tori think about someone else for a change, too.

We wait in the hallway for Mrs. Bridgewaters to gather her belongings. She walks us down the hall and then heads toward the main office.

"I'll see you ladies tomorrow," she says, then points to her diamond-studded READ pin. *Maybe I'll watch a little TV after I work on my writing assignment tonight.*

"Goodbye," we say together.

As we continue to walk down the hall, I notice that everyone's hands are full. *You know who's* reading a book. Not any book, her book. Leave it to Sabeen to write a book about...*whatever.* India's carrying a soccer ball, but she fell off her bike and fractured her arm and won't be playing in the soccer championship tournament. She's now the official ball girl. She told us she heard her mom say, "There goes that athletic scholarship." Tori's carrying a piccolo case because she wants to, and I quote, "expand my horizons."

When we get to the door, Sabeen stands next to me and says, "Let me do the honors. After you."

I'm in shock! Someone else besides me is holding the door for a change. Before I walk through the door, I hesitate and then read our school motto.

"Whatcha lookin' at?" Sabeen asks.

"Our school motto."

"What school motto?"

"That one," I respond, pointing to the TV monitor.

Sabeen reads aloud, *"At Three Rivers Elementary School we enter to do our best and we leave to help others."* She reads it again, this time slowly. She reads it a third time, under her breath. It is true, what teachers say, "Good readers *do* reread." Sabeen takes a step back and looks at me. "I've never read that before. I've never even seen it."

"For goodness' sake, Sabeen." I pause. "Let me be clear about something. I know you like to read a lot of books, but sometimes you have to read *outside* your books. What you just read, our school motto, that's how my dad lived his life." I sigh and say, "I think I will, too."

Sabeen's silent, which is unlike her—I mean that as a compliment. She's thinking over what I said.

"I like the way you think," she says.

Sabeen throws open her book and points to the dedication page. It reads: *This book is dedicated to my best friends, September, Victoria, and India.* She turns to chapter one. I've got goose bumps and lose my breath when she shows me. My eyes dance, hip-hop style, and light up, the same way the candles lit up at the candlelight vigil for Dad when I scan the first page.

"No way, that's awesome!"

"Is that interesting, or is that interesting?" Sabeen asks, hysterically.

"Is that a rhetorical question?" I hadn't realized I'd asked the question out loud until Sabeen looks at me in shock.

"It's interesting, all right. May I read it?" I ask.

"Oui—yes." As we swap my lavender bouquet for her book, images of all the people who care about me, everyone who's taken the time to help me become a better person stand out in my mind.

I—can't—believe it! I'm reading a chapter book while walking home from school, and Sabeen is just…well…walking home from school…seriously! What a weird day this turned out to be: The day I become an "inside" the book reader, and Sabeen becomes an "outside" the book reader. Just two blossoming readers!

"Sabeen."

"Yeah?"

"Where do ants go on vacation?"

"Ahhh..I don't know. Where?"

"They go to F-r-a-n-t-s."

Sabeen laughs and grabs my arm. "C'mon, September. Hey, guys, wait up," she says, catching up with the others.

It took a while, but I finally finished my letter to Mrs. Bridgewaters. I was pleased with myself; I wrote it without needing to chew gum. Who needs to chew gum to help them concentrate when you have a great imagination and a sharp mind? Here's what I wrote:

feb. 16, 2002

My Talents

Dear Mrs. Bridgewaters,

I was afraid of this assignment at the beginning of the year because I didn't feel that I had any special talents or best qualities. But I feel different now. I don't feel that I'm _____ or an _____ (I've stopped using these words to describe myself, I'll tell you what they are later) because it's not true. I have lots of talents and that's what I'm going to share with you in this letter.

First, one of my talents is that I'm good at helping people. I always hold the door open for my friends when we leave school because their hands are full. I'm also a greeter at my church and hold the door open for people when they come in. I like holding the door for people because it's fun and I like being helpful.

Another one of my talents is being a good friend. I think I'm a good friend because I support my friends by going to their games (even in the rain) and piano recitals. I even help them with their reading! I taught Sabeen how to pay attention to words outside of books and I'm teaching my friend, Tweet, who's eighty one years old, how to read. My pastor, Pastor Farmer, drives Nathaniel, his newly adopted son, and me to the Vintage Center on Saturday to read with Tweet. I've learned that you can teach an old dog new tricks if they're willing to try.

I've got one more talent up my sleeve. Do you know what it is? Well, I'll tell you: it's being a good listener. I love listening to people tell stories. They make me feel good when I hear them.

Oh, I almost forgot. I'm also a responsible person because I'm good at reminding my neighbors to clean up after their dogs when they take them for a walk and their dogs make uh-oh on the sidewalk. Our neighborhood secretary, Mrs. Willoughby, made me the neighborhood doggie enforcer person.

<u>My 3 goals this year:</u>
• speak up more often (especially at school)
• read books outside of school
• think positively about myself

Your friend,
September Champlin

P.S. Thank you for writing the letter to the president. That was the best thing ever!

P.P.S. Thank you also for opening my eyes to the incredible world of children's literature. Through it, I've found a kind of peacefulness I had never imagined. When I want to escape the craziness of my life, I simply read a book and I'm lifted to another place in time where I am ten feet tall... and happy.

Author Letter

It's long been known that books don't stand alone. They rest on and inform each other. Because of this relationship between books, the idea for writing this story came about after my reading Christopher Paul Curtis's book *The Watsons Go to Birmingham—1963,* published by Delacorte Press in 1995 and winner of the Coretta Scott King Honor Award and Newbery Honor Award in 1996. Inspired by his book, I, too, wanted to write a story that touches the heart and mind in deeply moving ways.

Though it took three years to write this story, the memories of our loved ones who died on September 11, 2001, will live on forever. To all those who lost a parent, relative, or someone special during the tragic events of 9/11, know that like books, you, too, do not stand alone...you will always have others to lean on.

And to all those children who read this story and identify with September's struggle with aliteracy—someone who can read but chooses not to—know that you as well can discover the rewards and lifelong fulfillment that books bring.

BH

"Be the change that you want to see in the world." ~Mahatma Gandhi

Books cited in *September's Big Assignment*

Jacob Have I Loved by Katherine Paterson

Zeely by Virginia Hamilton

M. C. Higgins, the Great by Virginia Hamilton

The Phantom Tollbooth by Norton Juster and Jules Feiffer

Bud, Not Buddy by Christopher Paul Curtis

The Piano Lesson by August Wilson

Shiloh by Phyllis Reynolds Naylor

The Slave Dancer by Paula Fox

Julie of the Wolves by Jean Craighead George

Roll of Thunder, Hear My Cry by Mildred D. Taylor

Aunt Flossie's Hats (and Crab Cakes Later) by Elizabeth Fitzgerald Howard and James Ransome

Love You Forever by Robert Munsch and Sheila McGraw

Abuela by Arthur Dorros

Where the Wild Things Are by Maurice Sendak

Dinner at Aunt Connie's House by Faith Ringgold

Chicken Sunday by Patricia Polacco

The Snowy Day by Ezra Jack Keats

Mufaro's Beautiful Daughters: An African Tale by John Steptoe

Cloudy With a Chance of Meatballs by Judi Barrett and Ronald Barrett

The Legend of the Bluebonnet by Tomie dePaola

JoJo's Flying Sidekick by Brian Pinkney

When I Am Old with You by Angela Johnson and David Soman

Thematic Questions for Group Discussion and Individual Contemplation

Questions shape the kind of knowledge students acquire. The questions that follow are designed to prompt students to thoughtfully obtain core themes and concepts related to the novel. They provide the breadth and depth necessary to develop a core mindset for twenty-first-century learning.

LITERACY

Aliterate:
• What do you think the term "aliterate" means? (It means someone who can read but chooses not to. If needed, give them a clue/hint like: "What does the letter 'a' do to the meaning of the word 'literate'?") Ask students to identify the evidence in the novel that suggests September is aliterate, and then speculate as to why she might have made this choice. What might keep someone from choosing to read? Distractions like TV, music, movies, and/or video games? Motivational reasons like uninterested in reading? Discuss how these concepts about literacy are shaped at home.
• September said, "I *can* read, I just choose not to, that's all." (p. 1). Have you ever made or heard someone make a similar statement? Describe the circumstances when the statement was made. Why do you think it was made?
• Explore possible reasons why the author did not make other characters in the story aliterate.
• Suppose September decided not to become a reader after all. Explain what her future might be like. What could she be like as an adult? Speculate on the kind of job she might have. How can being aliterate affect a young person's future?
• Imagine that September did read over the summer like her classmates. What might she have said during the group discussion at

the beginning of the novel and why?

• If September had always held a positive attitude toward reading, how might the story have been different?

• If you had a friend who didn't like to read, what would you do to encourage him/her to read? Explain why you would encourage them in these ways.

• List the consequences of being aliterate and share them with a classmate.

Illiterate:

• What do you think the term "illiterate" means? (It means someone who cannot read.) The author does not explain how September taught Tweet how to read, though we know she did. "I'm teaching my friend Tweet, who's eighty one years old, how to read" (p. 101). Describe how you think September taught Tweet how to read. What materials might she have used? Where might she have taught him?

• Find other stories that describe how a character teaches another character in the story how to read to compare the books. For example, in the story *Maniac Magee* by Jerry Spinelli, Maniac teaches his friend Grayson how to read. How does he teach him and what does he use? How might it be different from how you think September taught Tweet how to read?

• Why do authors write stories about illiteracy?

• Find other books about illiteracy and compare how authors use it in stories.

Literate:

• Discuss the factors that changed September's outlook on reading. Be specific. What role did her father, Tweet, Mrs. Bridgewaters, and Sabeen play in shaping her attitude toward reading at the end of the novel?

• Locate other stories about literacy and analyze the actions and behaviors of characters who are avid readers. Compare, for example, Sabeen's actions and attitude about reading with Amanda Beale's from *Maniac Magee*. How are they alike and different?

FRIENDSHIPS

• Talk about the importance of friendships with students. In your own opinion, does September understand the meaning of true friendship? Find inferences from the story to support your response.

• Why do you think September said, "I'm closer with Sabeen than I am with India or Tori" (p. 11)? What examples from the story back up your claim?

• Who would you have a stronger friendship with: September, Tori, India, or Sabeen? Why? Describe how each character's personality and physical traits may have an impact on your choice.

• In the story September says, "I don't know why I'm friends with Tori…the only thing we have in common is our curly hair" (p. 55). Do you agree with this statement? Why or why not?

• Would you have responded the way September did when Tori got hit in the face with the soccer ball? Explain your response.

• Imagine if the reverse had happened and September had been hit instead of Tori. How might things have been different? Rewrite the story using dialogue from this moment to the end of the chapter.

• In the story September says, *Could I have been friends with a white girl?* (p. 20), referring to her relationship with Tori. In your opinion, would September have been friends with Tori in Pittsburgh in the 1940s given that Pittsburgh was so racially segregated back then according to Judge Bridgewaters? Why or why not?

• Read other books like *A Friendship for Today* by Patricia C. McKissack to analyze the friendship between a black girl and a white girl during the mid-1950s. Describe how the relationships between the girls in both stories are the same and different.

• September develops a friendship with Tweet when she visits him in the Vintage Center. How important to the story is their relationship? Explain your answer.

FAMILY

• Engage in a discussion about the importance of family relationships with students. Examine whether or not the students think September has a good relationship with her parents. Do they have a similar relationship with their parents and/or caretaker?

• Describe September's mother's and father's personality and how they interacted with September. Did she seem to get along better with one parent over the other?

• Speculate as to why the author had September remember catchy sayings her grandmother said such as "choose your battles" (p. 18), "clothes don't make a person" (p. 39), and "think before you speak" (p. 52) but never gave her a speaking voice in the story. Did this add or take away from the story? What role did her grandmother play in the way September thinks about life?

• September jumped into her Uncle Raymond's arms thinking he was her father. "Daddy!...You did come home" (p. 78). How did you feel the moment September found out that he wasn't her father? Why?

• How do you think September will feel toward Uncle Raymond in the future? Provide examples from the story about September's personality to support your claims.

• How does September view her dog, Dee-O-Gee? Provide evidence. Is it significant to the story?

• September's church, Bethany Baptist, can be viewed as an extension of her family. What role did Bethany Baptist play in the story? Provide examples from the story to show its significance.

DEATH

• The topic of death is a sensitive area for some children and adults to talk about, so be sure that you and others feel comfortable discussing this issue before you proceed. Explain that death is a natural part of the life cycle. Have you had anyone close to you (i.e., parent, grandparent, sibling) die? How did you deal with it?

• September's father's death will change her family's lives forever, in part because of the way he died. How will life be different for September, her mom, and Uncle Raymond? How will it also be different for Nathaniel?

• September displayed different emotions after learning about her father's death—sadness, hurt, anger. Were you surprised at her reaction to her father's death? Why or why not?

• How did the author foreshadow September's father's death? How did you feel after learning he died?

• September is still grief stricken after she and her mother return home from the White House and she attends a support group. How helpful was attending the support group for September? Are you aware of other types of support groups that help children deal with crises?

• Mrs. Bridgewater's letter to President Bush mentioned that September was a lot like her father. How is September like him?

• The Oxford English Dictionary defines a crucible as: "a situation of severe trial, or in which different elements interact to produce something new." In what ways is September's life like a crucible experience? Provide examples in your response.

GROWING UP AND FINDING ONESELF

• Describe what September was like at the beginning of the story. Identify a time in your life when you felt that same way. How does

September change as the story unfolds? What prompted her changes? In what ways did you change and what impelled you to change?
• Is Mrs. Bridgewaters's decision to give September a writing assignment over the weekend at the beginning of the story a good one? Why or why not?
• How important to the story was Pastor Farmer's conversation with September about talents and special abilities? Why?
• Complete the talents and best qualities writing assignment. Use the checklist as a guide.
• In what ways are you like and different from September? Use a graphic organizer such as a semantic feature analysis or Venn Diagram to show your work. How important was receiving her classmates' notes when her father was missing to September? In what ways did the messages boost her self-confidence? Explain your response. How would you have felt?
• In your opinion, what was the most significant change that September made in the story? Why? What is her greatest talent or special ability? What is your greatest talent or special ability?
• What did September draw upon when she told Sabeen to "read *outside* your books" (p. 99)?
• Would she have said something like this at the beginning of the story? Why or why not?
• Debate whether September's decision not to tell her father about the chipmunk's escape from the trap was a good one. What would you have done?
• Explain the literal and figurative meaning when September said, "They seemed more concerned with gathering the information than doing anything with it" (p. 97)?
• In what ways did Mrs. Bridgewaters's conversation with September at the end of the story help change her attitude toward reading?
• Suppose you didn't like to read like September. Would Mrs. Bridgewaters's speech at the end of the novel have been convincing enough to encourage you to become a reader?
• Would you have been irritated by Mrs. Bridgewaters's pointing to her READ pin like September? Why or why not?
• If you could question the author about how the school motto was

significant to the story, what would you ask and why? Make a list of other encouraging school mottos.

TERRORISM

• According to Yahoo!News online, the September 11, 2001 terrorist attack killing nearly 3,000 lives is the most memorable event recorded on television in American history. The second event is the 2005 coverage of Hurricane Katrina on the Gulf Coast. Check reference books and materials for historical details of the attacks and other memorable events in American history.

• Terrorism is not a common topic for children's books. Describe how the author walked a fine line to tell the story of one family's ordeal of this tragic event. Be specific. Use examples from the story.

• How has the United States security system changed as a result of the attacks? What is Patriot Day and how is it observed? Research how people show respect for those who died during the September 11, 2001, attacks.

• The community showed respect by holding a candlelight vigil in honor of September's father and others who died. Why did the author describe what occurred during the vigil instead of the funeral?

• Were you surprised when September went to the White House? What images went through your mind when the president gave his speech and when the balloons floated into the sky?

For information on discussion questions linked to the school curriculum, visit Dr. Bena Hartman's website at www.benahartmanbooks.com. Thank you.

About the Author

Photo by James Jablonski

September's Big Assignment is Dr. Bena Hartman's first chapter book. Her first picture book, *Jasmine Can: Creating Self-Confidence*, published by Ferne Press in 2011, describes how a second grader named Jasmine overcomes the reading challenges she faces at school and at home. Dr. Hartman is a former classroom teacher, resource teacher, and assistant professor of literacy education. She taught countless classes in children's literature, methods and materials in reading, and research seminars. She enjoys a good challenge and competes with her own children by reading as many books as possible over the summer months…and always seems to come up short.